"Stop Trying to Run Me, Daniel! I'll Find My Own Job!"

Daniel was ominously silent and Lani lowered her eyes to the floor. But when he finally replied his tone was measured. "You're really leaning on me, princess. Remember what happened seven years ago."

"Is that supposed to be the ultimate threat? That if I don't toe the mark you'll kiss me? It just might work; it was a pretty bruising experience."

"No, Lani. I meant that if you push me I'm going to push back. When I get around to making love to you, princess, you'll enjoy it. So much so that you won't want me to stop."

BROOKE HASTINGS
is an avid reader who loves to travel. She draws her material from many sources: the newspaper, politics, the places she visits and the people she meets. Her unique plots, full of real people who meet love in many guises, make her one of the best new writers in this field.

Dear Reader:

Silhouette Romances is an exciting new publishing venture. We will be presenting the very finest writers of contemporary romantic fiction as well as outstanding new talent in this field. It is our hope that our stories, our heroes and our heroines will give you, the reader, all you want from romantic fiction.

Also, *you* play an important part in our future plans for Silhouette Romances. We welcome any suggestions or comments on our books and I invite you to write to us at the address below.

So, enjoy this book and all the wonderful romances from Silhouette. They're for *you!*

Karen Solem
Editor-in-Chief
Silhouette Books
P.O. Box 769
New York, N.Y. 10019

BROOKE HASTINGS
Island Conquest

Silhouette **Romance**

Published by Silhouette Books New York

America's Publisher of Contemporary Romance

Other Silhouette Romances by Brooke Hastings

Desert Fire
Innocent Fire
Playing for Keeps

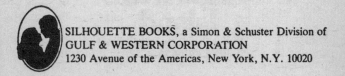

SILHOUETTE BOOKS, a Simon & Schuster Division of
GULF & WESTERN CORPORATION
1230 Avenue of the Americas, New York, N.Y. 10020

Copyright © 1981 by Brooke Hastings
Map copyright © 1981 by Tony Ferrara

Distributed by Pocket Books

ISBN: 0-671-57067-6

First Silhouette printing March, 1981

10 9 8 7 6 5 4 3 2 1

America's Publisher of Contemporary Romance

Printed in the U.S.A.

Island
Conquest

Chapter One

"Miss Douglas? Is there a Miss . . . uh . . . Kayoo . . . Kayoolaynee Douglas in the room?"

Lani looked up from her blue exam book, craning her neck from side to side in an attempt to see around two tall young men seated in front of her in the large auditorium. She had just finished jotting down notes for the answer to the last essay question of the last examination for her four years in college. One of the exam proctors was standing on the stage, his hand clutching a small slip of paper, his eyes darting around the hall in search of the woman he had paged.

Lani unzipped her purse and shoved her blue book and pen halfway inside, then made her way across twenty-two pairs of feet to the aisle. She rubbed her suddenly damp palms down the sides of her jeans, aware that her heartbeat had accelerated sharply. They didn't page people in the middle of finals except in the event of an emergency.

"I'm Kaiulani Douglas." The words came out in a whispered croak, Lani giving her somewhat fanciful name its proper Hawaiian pronunciation: Kye-oo-lah-nee.

The proctor, a graduate student, told her in a low voice, "You have a message to go to the Naval hospital in Balboa Park. Your father's had a heart attack, but he's alive." He held out his hand for Lani's exam booklet, his eyes roaming over her face and figure with a combination of sympathy and masculine appreciation. "I'll take care of that for you . . . I'll explain to Dr. Lopez. I'm sorry."

Lani nodded vaguely and drew the booklet from her purse. She was trembling with apprehension as she walked to her car and drove downtown to the hospital. Another heart attack! It was the third in six years for her stepfather. After the second attack Dr. Seaver had suggested an arteriogram—a test to determine the necessity for by-pass surgery. The results had been so encouraging that the doctors decided to rely on medication and diet to control the problem. Why had Jonathan suffered a third attack?

Once in the hospital, Lani gave her name to the receptionist and asked about her stepfather's condition. "Please have a seat, Miss Douglas," the woman said in a gentle voice. "Admiral Seaver asked me to notify him when you arrived." She volunteered no information on Jonathan Reid's prognosis.

Gene Seaver appeared some two minutes later, his stride characteristically brisk. The usual reassuring expression was absent from his face, however. The pallid cast of his skin matched his closely cropped gray hair; his normally infectious smile was wan and forced. He had been her stepfather's physician as well as his close friend for over ten years now, ever since Jonathan Reid was transferred from the naval base at Pearl Harbor in Hawaii to the base at San Diego, California.

Dr. Seaver was a professional optimist as well as an excellent doctor. Lani took in his defeated expression and had no need for verbal verification. Her stepfather, the only real father she had ever known, was dead.

She slid into his arms and sobbed on his shoulder, soaking his uniform jacket. "I'm sorry, Lani. I had to tell you in person," he murmured hoarsely.

He led her to his private office and, when she was calm enough to listen to the details of her stepfather's death, explained that they had been playing golf when Jonathan was stricken. "It was what we call a massive coronary occlusion. There was no warning, and no reason for it. He'd been doing so well the last few years." Dr. Seaver shook his head and smiled sadly. "We tried CPR and got him here as soon as it was humanly possible, but it was no use. He was on a hot streak, too. Best game he ever shot."

"At least he died happy. Don't blame yourself, Dr. Seaver." Lani felt as though she was standing some distance away observing her own attempt to console the kindly man sitting on the sofa next to her. In fact, she was more numb than shocked or grieved at that moment. In spite of Jonathan Reid's outward good health, some part of her had anticipated his death. How often had she tried to dismiss the sense of foreboding she had felt so frequently in recent months? She had told herself she was being panicky and pessimistic, but as it turned out, she was only being realistic.

"Do you want me to call Daniel for you?" Gene Seaver's gentle query broke into Lani's reverie. She politely declined his offer. Her defenses invariably slammed into place at the prospect of any contact with her stepbrother, Daniel Prescott Reid, but it was her duty to call him and she would do so.

His phone number was among those listed in the miniature black address book she carried in her purse. Although she invariably tried to avoid Daniel, she had feared that some day it would be necessary to make this call. She glanced at her watch; it was just past noon in California, and with the three hour time difference, Daniel would be in his Honolulu office by now. Lani picked up the phone on the end table and punched the O, followed by Daniel's phone number, instructing the operator in a surprisingly calm tone to charge the call to her home phone.

A charmingly accented voice answered, "Aloha, Prescott & Thomas. May I help you?"

"Daniel Reid, please." Lani suddenly shivered with tension, but felt that she was still in control of her emotions.

"One moment, please. I'll connect you with his office."

For several seconds Lani heard only the whisper of transpacific static. Then another lilting voice announced, "Aloha, Recreation Division."

"Mr. Reid, please. This is . . ." But Lani's explanation was lost in a burst of static. The receptionist said sweetly, "Mahalo." Thank you. "I'll connect you with his secretary."

Lani had no opportunity to voice her objections, because a moment later the secretary was on the line, repeating the greeting given by the receptionist.

Lani took a deep breath, and slowly exhaled. "Mr. Reid, please. Tell him Lani Douglas is calling." She wanted to explain further, but could get nothing more out. Now that she was faced with the task of telling someone else about her stepfather's death, she had to choke back her tears.

"Mr. Reid is in a meeting, Miss Douglas. Would you like to tell me . . ."

"It's personal," Lani interrupted. "Just let me speak to him." Her tone was hoarse, and impatient to the point of rudeness. Trust the high-and-mighty Daniel to make himself unavailable! The runaround Lani was receiving only added to her distress.

"I *am* sorry, Miss Douglass," came the firm reply. "Mr. Reid can't be disturbed. If you . . ."

"Yes he can be!" Lani sobbed. "You tell . . . you tell . . ." She was forced to stop by her breathless, gulping cries. Dr. Seaver removed the receiver from her hand, placing his arm around her shoulder while he spoke to the secretary. "This is Admiral Gene Seaver in San Diego. Mr. Reid's father died this morning. I was his physician. May I speak with him, please?"

Lani's sobs had subsided to shuddering whimpers by the time Daniel took the call. Dr. Seaver's tone was devoid of emotion as he relayed the news of Jonathan's death, only becoming husky as he added the medical details previously related to Lani. There was a brief silence before he held out the phone to her.

"He wants to speak to you. Will you be okay?"

She nodded, taking the receiver and mumbling into it, "Hello, Daniel. You don't have to come until the funeral. I'll take care of everything." As soon as the words were out she regretted the unwarranted insult they contained. Daniel was a loving and dutiful son

11

who had been close to his father in spite of the thousands of miles between San Diego and Honolulu. He had made a point of seeing his father at least three or four times a year.

Lani felt a rush of relief when she realized that Daniel had decided to spare her from an exasperated rebuke in favor of a measured reply. "I'll be in San Diego as soon as I can. You just take care of Brian until I get there, princess. Everything will be okay. Now put Gene back on."

Her face flushed with temper, Lani handed the phone back to Dr. Seaver. She was embarrassed whenever Daniel called her "princess," and resented his admonition that she take care of her little brother. After all, she had been doing so quite competently since his birth six years ago.

Her mother, Anne, had married Jonathan Reid when Lani was eight years old. Lani's real father, also a naval officer, had been killed in a service-related accident when Lani was only five. Since James Douglas had spent months at a time at sea, Lani had only the haziest memories of him.

It was natural that her mother and stepfather would wish to have a child together, but for years they were disappointed. When Anne finally became pregnant, she was already in her forties, but she was determined to bear the child. She endured a difficult labor which her doctor was forced to interrupt by performing a caesarian section. She never lived to see the son she so fiercely desired—she hemorrhaged to death.

Jonathan Reid had retired from the Navy the year before, and although both he and Lani were devastated by Anne's death, the necessity of caring for Brian helped pull them through a wrenching bereavement.

He was a beautiful, happy baby who looked very much like Anne. But perhaps the strain was too great for Jonathan, because several months after Brian's birth he suffered his first heart attack. Although Lani was only 16, she readily accepted responsibilities that might have crushed someone far older and more mature. Since it was summertime, she was able to be a nurse to her stepfather and still devote herself to taking care of her baby brother.

Over the last six years she and her stepfather had watched Brian grow into a self-sufficient, bright little dynamo. While Jonathan was recuperating from his second heart attack, Lani had help in the house: Daniel had insisted on paying for a nurse. But in general Lani had been the anchor of the family, and was much more like a mother than an older sister to Brian.

During those same years, she had finished high school and gone on to college. In her own mind, she had decided that one day Brian would be her exclusive responsibility. Her only concern was to prepare herself to support both of them. If she thought at all about the role of Brian's wealthy half-brother, it was only to pretend to herself that nothing would give her greater pleasure than for Daniel Prescott Reid to disappear into the depths of Kilauea volcano, to be followed by every one of his snobbish maternal relations. Not for the world would she admit to any more tender feelings toward her aloof stepbrother.

While Dr. Seaver talked to the man she fervently wished to sacrifice to the goddess Pele, Lani tried to concentrate on thoughts of her future. There would be some sort of military stipend for Brian, since he was her stepfather's minor child. Added to what she estimated she could earn, she would be able to manage.

Of course, there was the problem of day care, but she would work things out. She had to.

It was less agonizing to dwell on such practical matters than to remember that she would never see Jonathan Reid again. She ignored Dr. Seaver's hushed conversation with her stepbrother, shrugging out from under his arm when he hung up the phone. "I called Barbara earlier," he told Lani. "She should be over at your house by now. She'll sit with you until Daniel comes. I'll be over as soon as I can."

Lani thanked him, declining his offer to call a taxi and insisting that she would have no trouble driving back home to La Jolla. In fact, it was a harrowing trip. She was unable to keep her mind on her driving and as a result almost rear-ended three different vehicles.

As she pulled into the driveway of their three-bedroom ranch house, the salty tang of the nearby Pacific Ocean acted as a soothing narcotic on her battered emotions. Mrs. Seaver, a tall, slender woman in her mid-fifties, was leaning against the front bumper of her station wagon, waiting for Lani.

They entered the house arm-in-arm, and spent the next several hours drinking coffee and reminiscing about Anne and Jonathan, the good times and troubled ones. Barbara had already called a number of people with the news of Jonathan's death, and word would inevitably spread through their circle of friends. Mercifully, thought Lani, Barbara had asked that everyone stay away until tomorrow.

Brian returned home at three, walking from the near-by school he attended accompanied by two older children who lived on their street. He cried and clung to Lani when she explained that his daddy had died. He had known that there was something wrong with

14

Jonathan's heart, even if he hadn't really understood it. Once assured by Lani that there was nothing wrong with *her* heart and that she would never leave him, however, he calmed down and was able to eat the snack she prepared for him.

Dr. Seaver arrived at four o'clock and joined his wife, Lani and Brian in the living room, where they were watching television. Eventually Barbara fixed a meal, but no one ate very much of it. From time to time the phone rang—neighbors and friends had heard the news and wanted to know if they could help. Gene took the calls.

Brian fell asleep on the couch shortly after dinner, and Lani carried him to bed and tucked him in. Alone with the Seavers, she felt a compulsive need to talk about the future. Did they think she could get a good job? Did they know anyone who could take care of Brian? Who did she see about her little brother's survivor's benefits? When should she call the lawyer?

Gene Seaver turned aside these questions with professional smoothness, repeatedly warning Lani that she was becoming unnecessarily agitated. His reassurances only succeeded in making her more tense. Finally she burst into tears again, sobbing, "I have to make some decisions. Don't you see that? Why won't you help me?"

Dr. Seaver's response was to pull a bottle of pills from his pocket. "I know you don't approve of these things, Lani, but please, do yourself a favor and take one. Believe me, there's time enough to discuss the future when Daniel gets here. He'll take care . . ."

"I don't want anything to do with Daniel!" Lani cried almost hysterically. "And I don't want your pills, either!"

"Gene, please. Let me handle this." Barbara Seaver gathered Lani into her arms. "It's all right, darling. You have plenty of time to make decisions. It's natural to feel you have to have all the answers this minute, I know. But things will work out. I have confidence in you. You'll make them work out."

Barbara led Lani into the bathroom and went to fetch her a sweater while Lani washed her face and brushed her hair. She noticed dark smudges under her eyes; the red in her eyes, a result of all the tears she had shed, made her irises look a brilliant blue. She released her wavy auburn hair from its tight bun—the hairdo was cool and practical for the warm weather but was making her headache worse. It fell in soft waves to her shoulders, the red highlights brought out by recent weekends at the beach. Lani thought she looked dreadful—pale and pinched and puffy-eyed. Any objective observer would have studied her delicate facial structure, finely arched brows, small straight nose and sensually curved mouth and pronounced her as beautiful and fragile as the stem of an antique crystal wine glass. The impression was reinforced by her slender neck and small-boned, 5′4″ frame. The objective observer would have been much mistaken, however. Lani's deceptively vulnerable-looking appearance masked a fierce independence and stubborn strength.

These qualities enabled her to control her wild anxieties and accept the wisdom of Barbara Seaver's comments. Although Dr. Seaver had no success in coaxing her to swallow one of his little white pills, she did agree to take some aspirin and sip a glass of chilled white wine. She was finally beginning to wind down when she heard the sound of a car pulling into the driveway.

Daniel didn't bother to ring the bell; he simply let himself in with a key. Lani was guiltily aware of a stab of irritation at her late stepfather for giving his overbearing son a key to *her* home. The Seavers rose to greet him, and Lani watched stoically as he shook Gene's hand and kissed Barbara on the cheek. As always, he looked completely fit and much too handsome, his well-tailored tan suit having suffered no damage from the five-hour flight.

Lani fought down her reaction to his looks. He was over six feet tall, his lean, tautly muscled frame having changed little from his days as a college track star. She noted with surprise that there were a few gray hairs among the dark strands now. At thirty-two Daniel was a little young for that.

His face had a patrician, New England look about it. Or perhaps only Lani assigned this description to his slightly elongated face and rather thin, arrogant features. After all, among his ancestors were a New England Protestant missionary couple who had arrived in Hawaii during the first half of the nineteenth century. One of their sons had married well, eventually controlling vast quantities of land through his Hawaiian princess wife. The only indications of Daniel's relationship to Hawaiian royalty lay in the blackness of his hair and the ease with which his skin seemed to drink up the tropical sun. His eyes were a cool, metallic gray. At the moment, they rested on Lani.

Lani met his gaze, careful to keep her expression icy even though his presence disturbed her. Daniel's usual reactions to her ranged from polite concern to blazing anger, and if he was temporarily steeling himself to pretend a certain measured affection, Lani knew it wouldn't last. He walked over to the couch and sat down next to her, putting his arm around her shoulder and kissing her on the cheek. Lani held herself rigid in his embrace, seeking to convey to him that although she was tolerating his touch, it was distinctly distasteful to her. In fact, his closeness invariably sent her pulse rate soaring, and the thought that he might notice was dreadfully humiliating to her.

After several seconds of undeclared war it was obvious that Daniel had no intention of removing his arm from her shoulder. Lani, unable to cope with her reaction to his touch, flung herself up from the couch and stalked to the center of the room. She noticed the troubled look exchanged by the Seavers, but ignored it. After all these years, they knew that she preferred to avoid Daniel, even if they didn't know why.

Daniel rose as well, turning to the Seavers and saying crisply, "Thank you for looking after Lani and Brian. I can handle things from here on in."

Lani held her tongue until the Seavers were out the door, then let fly with a scathing attack. "I'm perfectly capable of *handling* things myself, Daniel. I'm the one who's lived with Daddy for the last fourteen years. And taken care of him for the last six. I don't need you or your money, and I don't want you here for a moment longer than you have to be!"

"It won't take long to wrap things up," he replied in a level tone. "You've had a tough day, honey. Go to bed."

"I'll do whatever I like! Don't you give me orders!" Lani flared. If Daniel had suggested that she stay and talk to him, she would have marched into the bedroom. He had that sort of perverse effect on her.

There was an exasperated sigh. "Don't push me, Lani. I loved my father, and I'm going to miss him. I'm in no mood to put up with that chip on your shoulder, not in these circumstances. Now get into that bedroom, or I'll carry you there myself."

Lani didn't doubt it. There was a grim curve to Daniel's mouth that told her not to argue.

She awoke early the next morning after a troubled night's sleep and quickly pulled on a robe over her baby-doll pajamas. Daniel and Brian were already dressed and had gone into the kitchen to eat breakfast. Snatches of their conversation reached her ears, prompting her to pause just outside the doorway to eavesdrop. They were talking about the most recent volcanic eruption on the Big Island—Hawaii—and Daniel had promised Brian that during the next such spectacle they would fly over for a closer look.

"Not if I have anything to say about it," Lani muttered to herself. Although Brian was Daniel's half-brother as well as her own, she told herself she had no intention of letting him steal the child away from her. She walked into the room, ignoring Daniel's "Good morning" and refusing his offer of an omelet with a curt shake of her head.

"Brian is going to school today," he said. It was a flat statement of fact. Daniel wasn't wasting any time in asserting his authority, Lani thought resentfully. She forced back her instinctive retort and looked at the child. "Is that what you want, Brian?" she asked gently, thinking that perhaps it was best if the child's routine remained undisturbed.

He nodded. "We're having a party. It's Jeremy's birthday today." Lani managed a smile, then bent down to kiss him. "Okay. If you want to come home, you call me, honey."

It was a relief to watch him kiss Daniel good-bye and run out the door to meet his schoolmates. It left her free to speak her mind to Daniel.

"What was all that about Hawaii? Brian isn't going to Hawaii; he's staying here with me." The aggressive challenge flowed readily from her lips, but Lani was far less confident than she sounded. The night before, as she was lying in bed trying to fall asleep, she had realized just how vulnerable her position really was. Her deepest fear was that Daniel Prescott Reid, with his money and his influence, was going to take her little brother away from her. Only now was she acknowledging to herself that she stood absolutely no chance against Daniel in this matter.

Her bravado failed her when it came to following up her uncompromising words with a haughty stare. She turned her back to Daniel to pour herself a cup of coffee, and heard the scrape of his chair as he pulled it out to sit down at the kitchen table.

"I would have preferred not to discuss Brian's future just yet, but since you've raised the issue, Lani, I'll give it to you straight. Brian is coming with me, and so are you. It's what Jonathan wanted and it's what I want. And if you'd calm down and think rationally about it, you would see that it's best for you, too."

It was a full thirty seconds before Lani trusted herself to reply. In other circumstances, perhaps Daniel would be right. But then, he could have no inkling of the effect he had on her, and did not know why she was so aloof and curt in his presence. How could she possibly manage to live in the same house with him? She carried her coffee over to the table and sat down opposite him, cursing the fact that her hand was trembling.

"Please don't do that." Her voice was husky with

apprehension. "Brian belongs here. His . . . friends are here. And his school. And . . . and me."

"What you really mean is that you don't want to come to Hawaii with me," Daniel translated softly. "I agree that Brian needs you, but if you won't come, I'll have to take him anyway. My father's will names me as his guardian, and I intend to fulfill that responsibility. I can't leave him in San Diego with you."

Lani felt a hot flush creep up her neck. At the same time, she was overcome by a wave of nausea, forcing her to take several shallow breaths to keep control. It never occurred to her to question Daniel's version of her stepfather's will. He was not the type of man who shaded the truth.

She buried her head in her hands in a gesture of agonized defeat. Not only did Daniel have money and power on his side, it seemed that he had the full force of the law as well. She should have realized that her stepfather would place Brian's future in Daniel's hands. He could give their little half-brother advantages Lani could only dream of providing. It wasn't fair.

Given her stubborn nature, she couldn't let the matter rest—not without one final attempt to change Daniel's mind. Swallowing her pride, she met his implacable gaze and begged, "Please, Daniel. Brian loves this house. Leave him here with me. I'll manage. Maybe . . . maybe you could help out."

"Do you know how much this house costs to run each month?"

Lani shook her head. Her stepfather had always handled their finances.

"Nearly one thousand dollars. I know because I own it. I also pay most of the bills." He folded his arms in front of his chest, his expression bland.

Somehow this revelation failed to surprise Lani. They had moved into this beautiful house only blocks from the ocean five years before. Lani adored the beach, and she knew that Jonathan had bought the house to please her. She should have guessed that Daniel had paid for it—it was far too expensive for a retired naval officer to afford.

Now Daniel continued, "I've decided to sell the house, Lani. We'll have a memorial service here if you like, clean up my father's affairs, and then *all* of us are going back to Hawaii. I'd like my father to be buried on Maui, next to my mother."

Lani was reeling from the force of too many blows, and this final setback destroyed her tenuous composure. "No!" she screamed. "You aren't taking him back there. He's not going to be with your mother and her prejudiced, snobbish family. Before I'd let that happen, I'd . . . I'd . . ."

But there was nothing Lani could do if Daniel insisted on having his way in the matter, and she knew it. She bolted out of the kitchen and into her bedroom, hurling herself down onto her bed and sobbing wildly. It was several minutes before Daniel followed. When Lani heard him enter her room she bit down on her lip in a desperate effort to control herself.

"Lani." Somehow she couldn't cope with the gentleness in his tone, and when she felt his hand on her shoulder, something inside her snapped. She jerked into a sitting position and attacked like a cornered animal, taking out all her frustration and grief on the man sitting next to her. Her hands curled themselves into fists and she began to punch wildly at his chest, tears rolling down her face.

Daniel simply grabbed her wrists and forced them

down into her lap, holding them captive with one large hand. The next moment she was pulled firmly onto his lap as he sat on the edge of the bed, her body enveloped in a relentless bear hug. Lani struggled impotently, demanding that he release her. Eventually, exhausted, she gave up and rested her head against his shoulder, crying softly.

Daniel's grip relaxed into an embrace, his hand lightly stroking Lani's back. There was a brief moment when he rested his head against her own, his lips lightly nuzzling her hair. Lani stiffened with shame at the rush of heat that tore through her body as a result of this innocently comforting action, and abruptly pulled away. She felt much calmer after her emotional firestorm—perhaps she had needed to explode that way—but if she had ever learned anything, it was to fight against the way Daniel so easily aroused her. Allowing herself to show such feelings would only lead to a repeat of that ghastly episode seven years ago.

Daniel permitted Lani to draw out of his embrace, but continued to hold her loosely about the waist, staring down at her with knowing amusement in his eyes. It was mortifying to her that he understood the reason for her hasty withdrawal.

"Don't look so outraged," Daniel murmured. "Put it under the heading of friendly comforting."

"You're not my friend," Lani mumbled, intensely conscious of the way his breath had fanned her cheek. "Please let me . . . ."

"Believe me, I have no desire to be your friend." Daniel lifted her from his lap to the bed, a mocking smile on his face. "Before you insulted my family and ran out of the room, we were trying to discuss funeral arrangements. You might have made your objections known in a less dramatic manner than a fullblown, frontal attack." He continued to hold her wrist firmly, forcing her to remain seated next to him.

Lani said nothing. Although Jonathan Reid had legally adopted her, she couldn't dispute Daniel's moral right to decide funeral arrangements. Part of her dislike of his mother's family stemmed from the manner in which they and their kind had ravished Hawaii. The rest of it was rooted in her awareness of how shabbily they had treated her stepfather after he married Daniel's mother. It was ironic that Jonathan Reid, who had been icily tolerated by the Prescotts while he lived, would join them in death.

"Not speaking to me, hmm?" Daniel had never taken his eyes from Lani's face; she hid her confusion by plastering a rebellious expression on her face.

After a rather dramatic sigh, he tucked a finger under her chin, forcing her to meet his eyes. "Okay, princess, you win. If you want him next to your mother, that's what we'll do."

Lani stared at him, amazed by the uncharacteristic concession. "Why? What made you change your mind?" she asked suspiciously.

"I'm giving you something you want in exchange for something I want," Daniel said teasingly. "You and Brian will come back to Hawaii, and live in my house. Let's not argue about it anymore, princess."

"I should have known. My feelings don't matter. It's always business with you, isn't it, Daniel?"

"If you say so. I admit that when I want something, I usually find a way to get it. It will be best for Brian, and best for you. Trust me, Lani."

Without waiting for her acquiescence, he rose from the bed and strolled out of her room. Lani's emotions were deeply divided. She loved Hawaii and had always longed to return to her home state some day. But she doubted her ability to disguise her feelings from Daniel, and if she slipped, she was going to make an even bigger fool of herself than she had seven years ago. It was one thing to put up barriers against a man she scarcely ever saw. But how would she manage when they were living together in the same house?

Chapter Two

Lani emerged from her room only after she realized that Daniel had closeted himself in her stepfather's bedroom, apparently to make business calls. She heard the muffled sound of his voice when she hesitantly poked her head out of her open door. Then she ventured into the kitchen, and had just poured herself a glass of juice when the doorbell rang. Barbara Seaver stood with her arms full of packages containing home-baked goods contributed by various friends, many of whom stopped by during the day to offer their help and condolences.

Funeral arrangements were left to Daniel. He decided against a military burial in favor of a simple church service and graveside ceremony to be conducted by their minister. Lani was informed of this immediately after Daniel's hushed conversation with Reverend Taylor, who had arrived late in the morning to offer what comfort he could to Lani. Although Daniel's plans were in accord with her own preferences, she would have preferred that he had consulted her first. Could she trust his gentle explanation—that he wanted to spare her the anguish of dealing with such painful details?

The weekend passed without further incident, primarily because the house was constantly filled with visitors and Lani was able to avoid being alone with Daniel. Usually she was defensively aloof in his presence, but from time to time over the last seven years she had given in to the urge to provoke him, not really understanding why she did so. When this happened, Daniel usually took her complaints literally, answering in a calm, reasoned fashion. But not always. Lani could remember a few occasions when her taunts had clearly found their mark, and his subsequent, rather frightening anger. The fact was, Daniel Prescott Reid intimidated her.

And now she was tense and unsettled whenever he directed his attention to her. At the same time, she was almost obsessed with protecting Brian from doubts and fears. She refused to let herself cry, feeling certain that if Brian saw her break down, his own anxieties would rage out of control. Many people commented on Lani's apparent composure, unaware that the perfect hostess was constantly struggling to maintain her self-possessed facade. By nine o'clock every night she was emotionally and physically exhausted, too wrung out to dwell on the future and too tired to do anything but fall into bed and sleep.

Daniel had not informed her of the specific arrangements for Monday's service, and Lani was too intent on avoiding him to ask for details. Thus, when they set out for church on Monday morning, she had no idea of what to expect. Daniel drove her car; Brian was tucked between them on the front seat. Lani smoothed an imaginary wrinkle from the matching jacket of her navy and white shirtwaist dress and reached over to return an errant strand of Brian's blond hair to its proper position. She glanced across at Daniel; his suntanned face was set into a composed expression which showed no signs of the wanness and dark semi-circles that Lani had hidden with make-up.

Always aware of Brian's small hand clutching her own, Lani sat stoically through most of the service. Her eyes grew moist when she listened to tributes from the minister and Dr. Seaver, but the handkerchief she carried remained in her purse, unneeded. Somehow it had never occurred to her that Daniel might wish to say a few words, and she was surprised when he rose to address the mourners.

His father, he said, had suffered two great tragedies in his life: the deaths of Daniel's mother, Laura, and of Jonathan's second wife, Anne. But he had also found great joy in the love and devotion of colleagues and friends. In a soft monotone, Daniel went on to thank many of them by name. Lani was impressed by his knowledge of his father's life here in San Diego, so far from the tropical paradise where Daniel made his home. She realized that Daniel and Jonathan must have been even closer than she had assumed.

Daniel continued his talk with a few words about Brian, saying that the child's birth had enriched Jonathan's last years and cushioned his grief over Anne's death. At the mention of his own name Brian began to whimper, and Lani pulled him out of his seat and sat him on her lap. She had been deeply affected by Daniel's reference to Brian, noticing how the increased huskiness of his voice contrasted with the rigid control he exercised over his features.

"But most of all," Daniel was concluding, "my father found comfort and contentment during the last years of his life because of Lani. She captivated both of us as a flame-haired little girl, and won our hearts as she grew up. She matured into a beautiful and devoted daughter who loved him and nurtured him and gave him strength. She has been as loving a mother to Brian as any woman could possibly be. I owe her a very great debt. Thank you, Lani."

For the first time, Lani reached for her handkerchief, dabbing at tears which could no longer be suppressed. As Daniel returned to his seat on the other side of Brian, she thought she saw his hand dart to the corner of his right eye to brush away a single tear.

After a brief graveside ceremony they drove back to the Seavers' house for a buffet lunch. No one spoke. Lani was pondering her stepbrother's emotional paean, still rather stunned that a man who had been so distant could profess admiration and appreciation for the loyalty and love she had shown his father. She was sure that any affection Daniel himself had ever felt for her must have vanished after that disastrous evening during the summer following her fifteenth birthday. Obviously he could disregard his own negative opinion of her character as a woman in assessing her qualities as a daughter and sister. If he was grateful, it was only because of Lani's devotion to his father and half-brother.

She found Daniel's praise unsettling and didn't understand why. What did it matter if his high regard didn't extend to her qualities as a woman?

After the majority of the guests had departed from

the Seavers', Daniel took Lani aside to explain to her that he was returning to Honolulu on business but would arrange for additional time off in order to help her settle her affairs. In spite of the sincerity of his tribute, she was relieved that he was leaving. Nothing would ever change the nervousness and defensiveness she felt in his presence. And now, she realized, she would probably feel guilty every time she opposed him. Clashes between the two of them seemed inevitable, and Daniel had admitted to her that he usually found a way to get what he wanted. Lani wondered if he assumed that his words of praise would assure her meek compliance with all his plans.

He arrived back in San Diego on Sunday evening, walking in just as Lani was tucking Brian into bed. He promptly took over the ritual of reading the child a story. Lani told herself that there was no point in protesting this usurpation of her role. In any event, she was tired, and well content to curl up on the couch and watch television.

Since most people had made their condolence calls in the days immediately following the funeral, the weekend had been a quiet one. With no one to entertain and most of the packing awaiting Daniel's orders, Lani was continually battling depression. She had arranged for Brian to play with friends for several hours each day, but when the two of them were alone she sensed that he was becoming increasingly unsettled about their forthcoming move. Their whole life would soon change radically, and neither of them had any idea of how well they would adapt. For the past six years, Lani had coped with crises by throwing herself into activity, but now she could do nothing but wait. She found it a great strain.

After saying good-night to Brian, Daniel joined Lani in the living room, sitting down next to her on the couch. Although he sprawled at least a respectable foot away from her, she was unable to prevent her body from stiffening defensively. If Daniel's mere presence was sufficient to disturb her, his closeness positively unnerved her. She was never able to relax in his presence.

"Brian seems to be doing okay."

Lani was grateful that he had chosen a safe topic of conversation. "He's so little—I don't think he really understands," she replied. "Sometimes he's sad or a little frightened, but basically he's looking forward to living in Hawaii . . . just as long as I'm with him."

Lani caught Daniel's nod out of the corner of her eye, and shifted her position so that she was turned slightly toward him and could glance up to catch his expression. At the moment it was pensive. "And you?" he asked. "How are you doing?"

Lani knew it was unwise to provoke Daniel, but somehow she couldn't help blurting out, "Oh, you know me. I'm a regular brick. Devoted and loving and nurturing, not to mention captivating!"

"I meant those things, Lani. And I *am* grateful to you. There's no reason . . ."

"Then let us stay here!" she begged. "Please, Daniel."

"No." The word was spoken softly but forcefully. "I know what's best for you. I'm sorry that you feel I twisted your arm, princess, but I'm going to have to hold you to our agreement."

Lani made no reply. She couldn't possibly explain her real objection, and if she argued with him he would probably lose his temper. She uncurled herself from the couch and murmured that she was very tired.

"I know it's been rough on you, honey," he answered sympathetically. "Once you settle down in Hawaii, you'll feel much better." He followed her up and walked off toward the kitchen.

It was not yet nine o'clock, far too early for Lani to be able to fall asleep. She tried to concentrate on a magazine article she had set aside to read some time ago, but eventually gave up. Her thoughts persisted in wandering to memories of her relationship with her formidable stepbrother.

He hadn't seemed so formidable the first time she met him. She had been only eight years old. The previous December a mutual friend had introduced her mother to Jonathan Reid; after a five-month courtship they had decided to marry. Lani had liked Jonathan immediately and couldn't wait until her future stepbrother came home, because only his absence was delaying the wedding. Jonathan would not marry Anne until Daniel could be present.

Lani remembered waiting in the airport in Honolulu for Daniel's plane to arrive from Los Angeles. It never occurred to her to ask why Daniel Reid attended what she later learned was an exclusive boys' prep school in New England. At eighteen years of age he was a distant figure, best compared to the boyfriends of her babysitters.

Like many little girls, Lani was unconsciously and charmingly flirtatious with men, and quite delighted with herself when Daniel began to use the nickname she now disliked—princess, for her namesake, Princess Kaiulani. Daniel treated her with amused indulgence, teasing and playing with her whenever they saw each other. His visits were frequent; although he had his own apartment, Anne Douglas Reid had extended an open invitation to her new stepson to come to dinner any time, and he took full advantage of it. Lani knew that he had a summer job at one of the hotels in Waikiki, but she never suspected that it was owned by his family.

He returned to school in the fall, this time to an Ivy League college in Massachusetts. Lani decided that Daniel must be very special, because the older brothers and sisters of all her friends attended college at the University of Hawaii's local campus. She was far too young to realize that although her stepfather earned a comfortable income as a naval officer, he was hardly in a position to afford the type of education Daniel was receiving.

Jonathan Reid's job was an administrative one, and when Lani was ten he was promoted to Captain and transferred to the naval base in San Diego. The only difficulty Lani experienced as a result of this move concerned her name. In the islands, everyone knew that Princess Kaiulani had been the heiress presumptive to the throne of Hawaii, the young woman who would have succeeded Queen Liliuokalani had the United States not annexed Hawaii in 1893. In San Diego, however, her name was thought to be exotic and bizarre, especially since Lani was a red-haired pixie with skin that needed gradual exposure to the sun if she was not to burn. After a few months on the mainland she gave up correcting mispronunciations of her name and accepted the fact that even her nickname would be butchered by people who insisted on rhyming it with Danny rather than Connie.

She saw Daniel only twice a year, in June and September, first when he stopped in California on his way to Hawaii and then on his way back to school in Cambridge, Massachusetts. Lani always looked forward to these visits because Daniel invariably spoiled her with gifts and outings, and could always be relied upon to ferry her and her friends to any destination they chose—even Disneyland, if they begged hard enough.

It wasn't until Lani turned thirteen that her girlfriends started chattering about how handsome her stepbrother was. Most of them had crushes on him, and at one slumber party they took a vote, ranking him just below the year's top teen idol. Lani relayed the compliment to Daniel the next morning, and suspected that he was rather put out that he had come in second.

Their praise was not undeserved, Lani admitted to herself. Daniel was movie-star handsome, of course, but what really enchanted her adolescent friends was a certain aloofness and reserve that made him seem alluringly mysterious. These traits failed to fascinate Lani. She accepted them as part of his personality. In any event, she told her friends, his visits were infrequent, so naturally he was rather distant.

Daniel had finished college, worked for several years, and when Lani was almost fourteen decided to attend business school. In the beginning of the following summer he stayed only three days with them, hurrying back to Honolulu and the responsibilities he had temporarily abandoned to attend school. It was long enough to leave Lani smitten with admiration. She had begun to date, a number of carefully supervised excursions to movies and school dances with boys her own age. These evenings usually ended with innocent good-night kisses, none of which succeeded in raising her blood pressure even slightly.

Her stepfather sometimes teased her about how rapidly she was growing up, and Lani had only to look in the mirror to know he was right. By the end of the summer, the transformation was complete. For her fifteenth birthday, her mother permitted her to purchase an emerald green bikini, and by August she filled out every inch of it. Her hair had darkened to a stunning shade of auburn and fell below her shoulders; her face had lost its rounded childish contours in favor of a sculptured beauty that made her look several years older than she was. She was secretly pleased at how often college boys tried to pick her up on the beach, but she knew enough to refuse them. She had heard what had happened to her friend's big sister, who had paid a heavy price for her lack of common sense.

Daniel returned to the mainland that same month, staying with them for a week and a half before heading back to the east coast for his final year of business school. After two days in Daniel's company, Lani was wholly infatuated with him. In the past, she had never exactly thought of him as a member of the family, but then she had never thought of him romantically either. Now her experiences with boys her own age made her aware of just how attractive he really was.

His behavior that August was no different than before, but Lani's reaction to it was. Every time they were together, her body flamed with longing. At first Lani was acutely embarrassed by this, but soon her newly awakened senses swamped her common sense and she began to yearn for a fulfillment she didn't really understand. She only knew that she wanted Daniel to notice her, to think of her, as she dramatically confided to her best friend, as a woman.

Unfortunately, Daniel seemed oblivious to the campaign she mounted. She dragged him to the beach and paraded around in her green bikini, making sure that her body often brushed his, constantly touching him, ostensibly to emphasize some point she was making. Once her mother caught her without a bra under her tee shirt and sent her back to her room to change, her cheeks crimson from the lecture Anne had delivered, right there in Daniel's presence.

When the first week of his stay ended with no progress toward her goal—which she pictured as a passionate embrace somewhere along the lines of Clark Gable kissing Vivien Leigh in *Gone With the Wind*—she accelerated her provocations. She was overwhelmed when Daniel finally accepted her insistent pleas that they go for an evening drive. He would be leaving in two days and she had almost given up hope of reaching her goal.

This time she was more clever about her attire. She donned a white, tank-topped tee shirt that left little to the imagination, hiding the sensuous result with a navy windbreaker. Her skimpy cut-offs molded her hips and bottom in an alluring fashion. At Lani's request, they drove to a secluded spot up in the hills, her excuse being that she wanted to show Daniel the view. When she emerged from the car, ostensibly to stretch her legs, the scenery he saw had absolutely nothing to do with the Pacific Ocean. She had removed her windbreaker and left it on the front seat. She yawned, lazily raising her arms and stretching, her full, high breasts jutting out against the thin material of the tank top.

Daniel had remained in the car, watching her. She knew all about the way he was looking at her—she had received similar hot stares from boys on the beach and found them rather disgusting. But when Daniel looked at her that way, it excited her wildly.

He leaned across the seat and called out through the open window, "Get in the car, Lani. We're going home." His voice was husky and tense.

She complied, tossing her hair and sauntering to the car to sit down only inches from him on the seat. She was pretending to be cool, but in reality her heart was thudding so uncontrollably that she felt faint. When Daniel put out his hand to return the car key to the ignition she quickly covered it with her own. "What's your hurry, Daniel?" she asked in an oddly breathless tone. "Isn't the sunset beautiful?"

Daniel leaned back against the seat, apparently staring at the sunset, ignoring the fact that Lani had begun to trail teasing fingertips back and forth along his arm, ruffling the dark hairs on it. Finally he turned toward her, his mouth set in a frown and his eyebrows lowered in anger. "You've been asking for this all week," he growled. "Better me than someone else!"

He made no concessions to her youth and inexperience, striking as rapidly as a rattlesnake. Lani was stunned by the roughness with which he pulled her into his arms. Before she could protest his mouth was on hers, her lips forced apart with brutal insistence, his tongue exploring the softness within with a punishing savagery that shocked and hurt her. She sat motionless, too frightened to struggle. And then the feel of Daniel's mouth changed, gentled. His hand slid under her shirt to caress her breasts, his fingers playing with her in a way that sent waves of heat tearing through her body. She couldn't resist the now-tender explorations of his tongue—didn't want to. With a low moan she began to kiss him back, aware that his embrace was gradually roughening again, but too aroused now to be afraid of him.

When he pushed her away, she was both confused and disappointed. Then she noticed his rapid, irregular breathing, and the anger on his face, and retreated to her side of the front seat. She watched apprehensively as he brought his features under control.

"I want you, Lani. I'm taking you to a motel." The

husky words hit her like a punch in the stomach. How could she have been such a little fool? Daniel wasn't a boy her own age, who would be satisfied with a few kisses. He was a grown man—and a very virile one at that.

She was far too inexperienced to know whether she had aroused him past the point where he could stop. The very idea of such complete intimacy terrified her, and she could manage only a shake of her head.

She flinched when he started the engine, digging her nails into the palms of her hands to keep from crying. She could feel Daniel's eyes on her as the car idled, and was trembling by the time he asked icily, "What's the matter, Lani? Don't you want to sleep with me?"

She shook her head again, too distressed to care that tears were now slipping out of her eyes. "Please, take me home," she begged wretchedly. "I don't want you to . . . to . . ."

Her shoulders were caught in a firm grip as Daniel turned her around to face him. "Right. If you don't want to be treated like a tramp, don't act like one. You're not a child any more, Lani. You can't turn a man on and then expect him to switch off when you change your mind. You're just lucky you decided to experiment on me, and not on someone else."

With that announcement he released her and put the car into gear. During the ride home neither of them spoke. Lani began to realize that Daniel had never had any intention of taking her to bed, that he had set out to teach her a lesson. How much of his anger—and his passion—had been feigned for just that purpose? She was so humiliated that she doubted she could ever face him again.

She managed to prevent herself from trembling as

they walked into the house. After a feeble excuse to the effect that she felt sick to her stomach, she fled to her room, where she pulled off her shirt and examined her body in the mirror. She was horrified to see a bluish bruise on one of her arms. What on earth would her parents think?

She pretended to be ill with an intestinal upset and chills during the next several days. These symptoms gave her an excuse to wear high-necked, long-sleeved nightgowns and explained her loss of appetite. Lying in bed all day, she had ample time to remember her flagrant behavior, and in retrospect she was thoroughly ashamed of how wantonly she had pursued Daniel. Perhaps if he had come in to talk to her she would have managed an apology, but he totally ignored her.

Just before Daniel left, he stopped by her room to say good-bye. Usually he gave her a smile and a peck on the cheek on these occasions, but now he only stared stonily at her and said in a withering tone, "I expect you'll make a rapid recovery once I'm gone, Kaiulani." With that, he stalked out the door.

Over the next several months, Lani began to question Jonathan about her stepbrother, but was always careful to sound indifferent and offhand. Previously, she had simply accepted Daniel's polish and sophistication as a part of his personality; it never occurred to her that these traits must stem from his mother's family. Now she was unconsciously looking for reasons to keep him at a distance, and the revelations about his background provided a perfect rationalization for her attitude.

Initially, Jonathan merely explained that his first wife, Laura, had been a Prescott, and that Daniel's schooling had been paid for by a personal trust fund established for him by his doting grandparents. He was being groomed to take his place in the family business, Jonathan remarked.

Lani had only been ten years old when they left Hawaii, but she had already learned about the Prescotts and the Thomases in school. Along with a handful of other powerful local families, they had made a fortune in sugarcane during the nineteenth century. With the profits from that venture they had invested heavily in other island activities, from agriculture to real estate to shipping, from light industry to tourism, until they dominated the commercial life of Hawaii.

Even as a child Lani had resented the results. As Honolulu became a major Pacific city and Hawaii a favorite retreat for vacationers, the tropical beauty of the area slowly fell victim to a relentless procession of bulldozers. Lani equated development with avaricious destruction and in her own mind Daniel Prescott Reid was soon assigned the role of a ruthless, irresponsible industrial warlord.

She next saw him during Easter vacation, when he flew to the West Coast to spend the holiday with her family. Her mother was in the final trimester of a difficult pregnancy, and had been ordered to stay in bed because of the risk of a premature birth. Jonathan, who had retired the previous fall, spent most of each day at his wife's side. His efforts at cooking and housekeeping ranged from inept to disastrous, so Lani took over almost all of these responsibilities.

She reacted to Daniel's presence with a mixture of brittle defensiveness and pretended aloofness. She was afraid of being hurt—afraid of making a fool of herself all over again. In any event, it was obvious to her that Daniel wanted absolutely nothing to do with her, because from the minute he set foot in San Diego, he was careful to avoid her.

Two months later Anne Reid was dead, and three months after that Jonathan suffered his first heart attack. Daniel flew in from Hawaii on both occasions. Lani responded to his pro forma expressions of sympathy with cold civility, and took full advantage of the fact that the care of her infant brother provided a convenient shield to hide behind. Only once was she trapped into being alone with him, after Jonathan's heart attack; he had barged into her room just before leaving for Hawaii. He insisted on paying for a full-time housekeeper, but Lani angrily rejected the idea, saying that she wanted nothing to do with his filthy money and that she could manage perfectly well on her own.

Daniel had seized her arm and pulled her against him. For several moments they had stared at each other—steel-cold gray eyes meeting furious blue ones. Then he had cursed under his breath and turned on his heel, stalking out of the room.

Over the next several years, Daniel usually managed a week's vacation with his father in San Diego in addition to occasional business trips to the mainland. Although Jonathan took Brian to Hawaii each winter, Lani never joined them. She told her stepfather that she needed this yearly vacation from her little brother, an explanation he readily accepted.

At the age of twenty-nine Daniel was promoted to the Vice Presidency of Prescott & Thomas's Recreation Division. Lani added his new position to her list of grievances. Her occasional gibes as to his role as chief despoiler of the islands were invariably met by patient defenses of the importance of tourism to Hawaii's economy. But she still remembered the time she had gone just a little too far, and the blistering set-down she had received as a result. She had never again challenged him that way.

Although Jonathan made an excellent recovery from his first heart attack, he never regained his former energy and stamina. Lani's time was spent in school or at home, taking care of the house and looking after Brian. Although her physical beauty could be intimidating to young men, her warm, approachable manner encouraged invitations from them. Sometimes she accepted, but usually she was simply too tired to go out. None of her boyfriends made any deep impression on her or aroused her to the point that she wanted any deeper, more physical involvement.

In her more honest moments, she knew she was comparing every boy she dated to Daniel. None of them made her feel that wild abandonment she had experienced during those brief moments in his arms. Undoubtedly he had long ago dismissed the entire incident, but Lani never could.

For the past several years he had been polite yet distant with her during his visits to California, careful to inquire how she was managing and often offering his help, but never pressing her. She couldn't blame him for being aloof—every time he came too close, she stiffened with alarm. She reacted to any show of friendliness by coldly withdrawing, wary of Daniel but even more wary of her own, wild emotions.

In time, Jonathan confided the full story of his first marriage to Lani. He had met Laura Prescott just after the war, when she was in her middle twenties and had long ago lost count of how many wealthy bachelors had proposed to her. Under pressure from her parents, she was about to accept an engagement ring from a suitably upper-class man.

Jonathan had tried to pick her up on the beach, and Laura had been amused enough to permit it. Within weeks both of them knew they would become husband and wife. When Laura introduced the handsome but ordinary naval officer to her family, they were appalled. They vehemently opposed the marriage and cut their daughter off without a penny afterward.

This ostracism was abruptly relaxed after Daniel's birth. Jonathan characterized his in-laws' subsequent behavior as correct but frigid. Only Daniel received their loving approval—from the day he was born, he was spoiled not only by his grandparents, but by his uncle and aunt and their two teenaged children.

The Prescotts immediately established a generous trust fund for Daniel, so that by the time he reached his teens he was wealthy in his own right. The elderly Mrs. Prescott survived her husband by six months, dying when Daniel was twenty-eight. She divided her fortune evenly between her son, Daniel's Uncle Charles Prescott, and Daniel, who was the only descendant of her daughter, Laura Prescott Reid.

Given his money and position, not to mention his devastating good looks, Daniel became the target of every marriageable woman in his social set, a fact which greatly amused his father. After each trip to Hawaii, Jonathan would regale Lani with stories of how ardently poor Daniel was pursued, prompting her to observe acidly that she doubted he ran very fast. She was not amused to learn from Jonathan that Daniel usually checked up on whether she was involved with anyone. No doubt if she had behaved the way he seemed to, he would have labeled her as shamefully promiscuous.

She added this double standard to her list of grievances against him, And now, she thought unhappily, she was being hauled off to Hawaii, to face the snubs of his family, the patronization of his women, and the domineering manner of Daniel himself. She would have to remember all her reasons for keeping him at a distance, because she was very much afraid that in the tropical paradise of Hawaii, the summer sun would thaw all the ice she had so carefully buried herself in.

Chapter Three

On Monday morning, Daniel took Lani to the office of Jonathan Reid's attorney, Robert Epstein, to discuss the contents of her late stepfather's will. She learned that once her mother had married Jonathan Reid, all payments made to Lani as a result of her father's death had been invested for her. After fourteen years, this had grown into a sizable nest egg.

With the exception of a number of items willed specifically to Lani and bequests to various charities, Jonathan had left his entire modest estate in trust for Brian with Daniel named as guardian and trustee.

"Your father changed his will five months ago, after completing payment for your education, Lani," the attorney explained. He cocked an eyebrow toward Daniel. "My understanding is that he discussed the matter with you on his last visit to Hawaii?"

"That's right. He was afraid that I might railroad

Brian into the Prescott family business," Daniel said with a thin smile, "and I assured him I would invest Brian's money and turn over control to him when he reaches twenty-one. My father wanted him to have some independence."

"Lucky Brian," Lani inserted sourly. Certainly she approved of her stepfather's logic—she had no need of his money, especially in view of her own newly discovered assets. She only wished that Jonathan had trusted her enough to give her guardianship of Brian, but then he had had no idea of how she felt about Daniel. Naturally he would assume that she would be enthusiastic about returning to her home state.

"Please don't think your stepfather wasn't concerned about you, Lani," Robert Epstein told her. Obviously the attorney had misinterpreted the reason for her sarcastic comment. "He felt that once you graduated, you would be capable of earning your own living. And of course, your stepbrother had promised to be responsible for both of you. I'm sure that Jonathan never doubted your fitness as a parent for Brian, he simply felt that you had sacrificed enough of your life already. He told me that if you married he would reexamine his thinking on the matter, but as long as you remained single, he felt that both of you should make your home with Daniel."

Daniel was lazing back in his overstuffed leather chair, apparently amused by Lani's tight-lipped expression. "So the two of you arranged *my* future as well as Brian's," she accused angrily, "and you never considered consulting *me* about it!"

Daniel shrugged. "What was the point? You would have objected." He stood up and reached across the desk to shake the attorney's hand, effectively preventing any further arguments from Lani.

"Thank you for your time, Robert. I appreciate your handling things on this end. Keep in touch about the house."

Lani rose as well, repeating her stepbrother's handshake but limiting her comments to a cool thank you. There was nothing to be gained by airing family quarrels in front of the attorney. Her resentment was directed at Daniel, not at Robert Epstein.

Daniel took her arm and led her out of the one-story building. As soon as they reached the parking lot she pulled away and said in a low, husky tone, "You and Daddy arranged all this, didn't you? Neither of you wanted to give me any choice about what I would do if he died! Why?"

"We both felt that you and Brian should make your home with me. You're the . . ."

"How convenient for you that Daddy died," Lani spat out viciously. "If he . . ."

Daniel clamped his fingers around her upper arm and spun her around with enough force to leave her breathless, frantically inhaling the salty air. After a single, brisk shake he said furiously, "One more smart crack like that and I'm going to take a belt to your backside. I loved my father. Four years ago he agreed to move to Hawaii as soon as you finished college. And if you think there's any way I'm going to let you stay here alone, think again!"

"For heaven's sake, Daniel, I'm twenty-two years old. I'll do whatever I want to do!" Lani wriggled out of his grasp and stalked off toward the car, but found that Daniel had locked it. She felt like an idiot as she stood next to the front door, waiting impatiently for him to catch up with her.

When he reached her, his anger was unmistakable. It was visible in the rigid way he held his body and in the grim squint of his eyes. She noticed that he kept his hands thrust into his pockets, as if not trusting himself to leave her alone. "Don't ever walk away from me again," he ordered. He unlocked the door, slamming it shut as soon as she was seated.

Lani already regretted her sarcastic comment about Jonathan's death. It had been an unforgivable thing to say to Daniel, and she knew she owed him an apology. But he looked so furious she wondered if he would accept it. Her "I'm sorry, Daniel" was a mere whisper.

He nodded curtly. "Right!" He continued to hold the car key in his right hand, making no move to insert it into the ignition. He was staring out the windshield, still quite enraged with her, and Lani wondered if he allowed his temper such free rein in his business dealings. She doubted it.

Perhaps, she decided, she could tease him out of his black mood. After all, she was about to move into his home, and couldn't continue this constant battle.

"Daniel," she purred, "don't you think I'm a little too old for spankings?"

He glanced to his right, took in her broad smile, and quite deliberately let his eyes roam over her body, his appreciation all too obvious. "There are only two ways to control a woman like you, princess. The first is to beat her. Of course, I've never tried that. The second is to make love to her. As I remember, that works fairly well. Any preferences for the future?"

Lani felt her face heat up with embarrassment. Blast the man for reminding her of how effectively the latter method of punishment had handled her seven years ago! She refused to let him have the last word. "If your beatings are as painful as your way of making love, count me out of both!" She tossed her hair and stared poutingly at him, waiting for the inevitable mocking retort.

But he only smiled, slowly shook his head, and started the car.

Lani was amazed to find that the next few days passed without a harsh word or angry grimace. Daniel helped her pack, assuring her that he had plenty of room in the attic of his house for anything she wished to keep. She knew that he was eager to return to Hawaii as soon as possible to supervise the shakedown period for Prescott & Thomas's newest hotel, which had opened the day before Jonathan's funeral, and yet he never seemed impatient when she had difficulty in making a decision about how to dispose of some cherished item. The Maunalua Bay Hotel, she learned, was the reason he had flown back to Hawaii on Monday afternoon, and not a day went by without a phone call from its manager.

Even so, when Brian begged for a trip to the San Diego Zoo on Tuesday afternoon, Daniel readily complied, telling Lani that they could finish packing that night. It was obvious to her that Brian idolized his big brother, but she felt no jealousy. How could she, when the three of them had spent such a delightful day together?

To Lani's relief, Daniel was friendly but impersonal, saving his hugs and kisses for an ecstatic Brian. She told herself that as long as he kept his distance, she would manage to live amicably with him. She allowed herself to hope that he would understand that she had led her own life for seven years now, and valued her independence. She would simply have to learn to control her physical reaction to him.

They flew to Los Angeles early Wednesday afternoon, picking up Brian from his final half-day of school in order to make the plane. Lani was amused when they were met at the airport by a trio of middle-aged men, all of whom wore an assortment of gold jewelry around their necks. Daniel had mentioned that they were from a television production company which had developed a series about a Hawaiian resort hotel. They wanted to shoot the pilot at Prescott & Thomas's new Maunalua Bay.

Daniel disappeared into an airport conference room with the Hollywood trio, and Lani passed the hours until departure time by taking Brian for a long walk around the airport, buying him lunch, and reading him stories.

The flight to Honolulu was an uneventful one. Lani and Brian sat in the front of the first class section; Daniel was directly behind them, working. Eventually Lani started to talk to one of the flight attendants, a girl in her early twenties who had also grown up in Honolulu. When she found out that Lani was a native Hawaiian who was returning after a twelve-year absence, she laughingly cautioned her about the changes in their home state. The girl found it an improvement. She enjoyed the bustle of activity during the daytime and the availability of entertainment at night, not to mention the increased numbers of handsome young men who surfed at Waikiki Beach each day.

The pilot landed the jumbo jet with silky precision. After deplaning, they walked down a flight of steps and were greeted at the bottom by a smiling young man whom Lani judged to be about her own age. He was several inches shorter than Daniel, with equally dark hair and eyes a darker shade of gray. Instead of the bronzed skin of her stepbrother, he sported an uncomfortable looking sunburn.

Slung over his arm were two flower leis constructed of purple vanda orchids, dozens of the little blossoms strung closely together. Most of the passengers from the flight had received no such welcome, and were proceeding directly into the shuttle trams that would take them to the baggage area. However, the members of a large group that had traveled with them were also being adorned with leis made of less expensive flowers: carnations and plumeria.

Daniel grasped the younger man's outstretched hand. "Tommy, thanks for meeting us. This is my little brother Brian and my stepsister Lani Douglas. This is my cousin Tommy Prescott, Lani."

Tommy bent down and placed one of the leis around Brian's neck, giving him the traditional kiss on each cheek along with the greeting of "Aloha." Then he rose and smiled at Lani, but before he could repeat the procedure, Daniel intercepted him, smoothly removing the lei from his arm.

He walked to within inches of Lani, placed the lei over her head, and gently lifted her hair to fan it out over the flowers. When he placed one hand on each side of her waist, she instinctively stiffened, her hands flying up to push lightly against his chest. Daniel bent his head, kissed her just in front of her left ear, slowly trailed his mouth across her face to nuzzle her lips, then continued across her right cheek to bestow a lingering kiss against the sensitive part of her neck just below her right ear.

The teasing sensuality of it left Lani breathless and confused. There was no doubt that Daniel had deliberately sought to arouse her, and his triumphant smile told her that he was well aware of how thoroughly he had succeeded. Her hands had curled themselves into tight fists that clutched his suit jacket; he unfolded them into his own hands and eased them down. "Welcome home, Kaiulani," he murmured, and then added with a grin, "Was that gentle enough for you?"

Lani pulled away from him, embarrassed by the intensity of her response to what she suspected was no more than impulsive teasing. Two could play *that* game, she told herself!

She flounced off toward his cousin Tommy, slanting him an inviting smile. "Don't I get a greeting from you, too?" she asked seductively.

He needed no further encouragement, placing his hands on her upper arms and kissing each cheek. After a quick glance at Daniel's stony expression he winked cheerfully at Lani and took possession of her mouth, letting his lips remain on hers for several seconds.

"I left the car in the garage," he told Daniel. "Why don't you take Brian for a ride on the tram to the baggage claim area while I take Lani to the car? I'll meet you outside."

Brian immediately began to pull Daniel toward the tram, and he had little choice but to follow, his gray eyes frosty as he told his cousin, "All right. Just remember that she's my sister, not one of the *haole wahines* you like to amuse yourself with, Tommy!"

Tommy only laughed. "Look who's talking. You take your pick of the mainland women and we get your rejects. Besides, she's not really even related to you." He took Lani's arm and followed Daniel and Brian out of the building.

"Is there something between you two that I should know about?" he asked as soon as they were out of earshot. "From the way my cousin kissed you, I'd say he'd like to do a whole lot more. But if I'm wrong, I'd like to take you out some time."

"And I'd love to go," Lani said, keeping her voice neutral. "Daniel has an odd sense of humor sometimes. The truth is, we aren't close at all." She studied the large buildings to her right and the parking structure to her left. "I don't recognize this place. There used to be a small terminal here. It was surrounded by flowers . . . it was beautiful. Now it looks just like the mainland."

"The new terminal was built in the mid-seventies. With the increased traffic from tourism and business, we needed a better facility."

As they approached the car, Lani grimaced. "Maybe bigger. Definitely not better." She pointed to a large, dark blue Mercedes-Benz. "That's a pretty nice car you've got."

"I drive a Porsche," Tommy grinned. "The Mercedes belongs to Daniel. I left my car at his house and picked this one up. We'll need the extra room for the luggage."

As he helped her into the car, Lani asked curiously, "What do you do? For a living, I mean?"

"I don't want to sound conceited, but I could retire to Fiji if I wanted to," Tommy told her. "Actually, I just finished college. I start law school next fall."

"Don't tell me," Lani groaned. "Harvard."

Tommy shook his head and laughed. "That's Daniel's alma mater, not mine. I went to Yale as an undergrad and managed to get into their law school, too. I figured that no one could compete with Daniel when it comes to running Prescott & Thomas—he's a shoo-in to take over the presidency when my father retires in ten or twelve years. I'll be satisfied to run the legal department someday." He glanced over his shoulder as he backed out of the parking space, catching the stormy frown that had appeared on Lani's face the moment he mentioned Prescott & Thomas.

"Hey, what's the matter? Did I say something wrong?"

Lani thought to herself that if she was going to have anything to do with Tommy Prescott, he might as well know how she felt about his family. "I'm going to be honest. I think the Prescotts are snobs. I hate what they've done to Hawaii, and I've heard that they were horrible to my stepfather the whole time he was married to his first wife."

"And Daniel?" Tommy prompted. "Why don't you get along with him?"

Lani couldn't very well tell him the real reason, so she parried lightly, "Maybe he's just too blue-blooded for me. It could be those royal ancestors of yours! Anyway, the reason I came to Hawaii was so that Brian could be with both of us. Daniel has custody, but I could never leave him. I've been like a mother to him for the last six years."

Tommy finished backing the car out and shifted out of reverse, speaking to Lani as he drove from the garage. "Don't judge the family by my great-grandparents. The old lady's name was Victoria—we used to call her The Queen—because heaven knows she acted like it. The old man was only slightly better. But they were born in another century, Lani. To them, the only acceptable marriage partners were from old Hawaiian families—*kamaainas*—or maybe New England blue bloods. My Aunt Abigail, Daniel's first cousin . . ."

"Wait a minute!" Lani laughed. "I'm a little confused about your relatives."

"That's not surprising," Tommy admitted. "Pay attention, and I'll try to straighten you out. Although it may be hopeless," he joked. "Victoria and Thomas Prescott had two children. One of them was Laura Prescott, Daniel's mother. The other was Charles Prescott. My father Richard and my Aunt Abigail are Charles' children . . ."

"Daniel's first cousins," Lani inserted.

"Very good! Which makes me Daniel's first cousin, once removed. And what I started to tell you is that when Aunt Abby married a Texas heart surgeon named Howard Regan, you would have thought she'd run off with a Cossack warrior. Uncle Howie was only really welcomed into the family fold after he operated on one of old Thomas's cronies and saved his life. Unfortunately for your stepfather, the best he could do was survive Pearl Harbor and get himself decorated as a naval hero."

Lani had to smile at Tommy's sardonic tone in relating this slice of family history. "I see. You're really just like anyone else, aren't you, Tommy? Just plain folks?"

"I can't honestly say that," he laughed. "I have to admit that old Charles was a bit of a tyrant in his time, but he's in his seventies now and he's mellowed. My father tends to be pretty easy-going, and even though my mother is a Thomas, you'll love her. Everyone does. As for Daniel, I wouldn't have the nerve to bait him if he weren't my cousin—I'd be afraid of landing on his blacklist. I think he's a throwback to the old lady."

They pulled up in front of the building housing the baggage claim area, but it was several minutes before Daniel appeared with Brian. While they were waiting, Tommy asked nonchalantly, "Does Daniel know how you feel about Prescott & Thomas?"

"He ought to," Lani muttered. "I haven't made any secret of it."

A moment later Brian opened the door and climbed into the back seat, bouncing up and down several times until Tommy finished helping Daniel load the suitcases into the trunk. Daniel got into the back with Brian, leaning forward soon after they left the airport to ask his cousin, "How come you're not taking the H-1?"

"I thought Lani might like a tour of the city. It's changed since she lived here." Lani wondered why he was grinning from ear to ear.

"Terrific. Just what I need, Tommy," Daniel said in exasperation. Then he added coolly, "Keep it up, and I'll banish you to work on Maui this summer." Lani had no idea what he meant.

Their route went through the industrial area surrounding Nimitz Highway, passed by the large Ala Moana shopping center, and intersected with Kalakaua Avenue. By that point, Lani noticed, Brian had fallen asleep. It was past midnight in California.

Although the city was far more developed than she remembered it, she was not overly distressed by the change—until she saw Waikiki. She remembered a wide beach with a limited number of hotels, each of them surrounded by beautiful gardens. The area had been transformed into a concrete jungle, with every available square foot covered by hotels, stores, offices and housing. As far as she was concerned, it was a clear-cut case of environmental rape, perpetrated by people greedy to make fast money from the state's burgeoning tourist industry. She was horrified.

"Daniel," she breathed, turning around to look at him, "what's happened to this place?"

"Want me to show you which ones belong to Prescott & Thomas?" Tommy asked, obviously enjoying himself.

"Quit it, Tommy . . ." Daniel growled, only to be

cut off by Lani's blistering attack, "It's disgraceful! You *kamaainas* don't care what you do to these islands as long as it makes all of you rich, do you, Daniel?"

Daniel cursed under his breath, then asked his cousin icily, "Did I say Maui? Make that Molokai, Tommy. No women. No nightclubs. Got it?"

Tommy held up one hand in supplication, keeping the other on the steering wheel. "Okay, okay. I'll set her straight," he said, and went on, "just let me work at the Maunalua Bay." To Lani, he said solemnly, "Miss Douglas, I've got to make it clear that your stepbrother is the embodiment of enlightened development. Since he took over as Rec Division Vice President, Prescott & Thomas goes in for the classiest projects in the islands. Wait until you see our new hotel—it's just past the Kahala district."

"But it used to be so beautiful out there," Lani cried, "so peaceful. The grass and the trees and the beach . . . you mean it's all gone?"

"All gone," Tommy agreed. His mischievous streak obviously got the better of him, because he added, "There's a terrific eighteen-hole golf course—too bad about the trees we had to rip out. And the view—the cliff had to be leveled and the area graded to put in a beach. And then there's the parking lot . . ."

"Molokai," Daniel interrupted, "as a volunteer in the leper colony."

Lani glared at her stepbrother, so utterly distraught at the change in her beautiful hometown that all caution or common sense had disappeared—far more rapidly than the lovely gardens of Waikiki ever had. "You'll destroy every inch of these islands before you're through. How *could* you, Daniel?"

Tommy gave a hoot of laughter, seemingly undeterred by his cousin's cold anger. "She's got you

wrapped around her little finger, doesn't she, Daniel?"
He looked over at Lani. "If anyone else had made a
crack like that, he would have taken her head off. Or at
least banished her to Molokai," he teased.

"Lani would love to live on Molokai," Daniel
informed his cousin. Lani was relieved at the note of
amusement in his voice. "Her idea of punishment isn't
the same as yours. She knows that I'll deal with her in
private, don't you, princess?"

Lani's shudder was quite involuntary. She had no
idea what Daniel planned to do to her, but was certain
it would be unpleasant. They were on Kahala Avenue
now, driving through an area that contained some of
Hawaii's most beautiful and expensive homes. Tommy
slowed the car as they drove parallel to a white stone
wall, then turned through a pair of open gates into a
wide driveway.

Lani's first reaction was intimidation at the size of
Daniel's home. It was easily twice as large as her own in
San Diego, a long, two-story rectangle with a second-
story balcony and a pitched roof covering an additional
half-floor—the attic, Daniel mentioned. The house
appeared to have been transplanted intact from a
colonial township in far-off New England, contrasting
oddly with the tropical plants that bloomed so profusely
in the flower beds and beautifully landscaped grounds
surrounding it. The light from the porticoed front
entrance joined the moonlight to illuminate a stunning
array of crimson reds, oranges, pinks, lavender blues
and yellows. The green shades of foliage and grass were
mirrored in the house's shutters, but its clapboard sides
were painted a stark, no-nonsense white.

Tommy swung the Mercedes into the oval turna-
round that arced to within twenty feet of the front
entrance, then stopped. "Open the door for me,

Tommy. I'm going to carry Brian inside," Daniel instructed.

They walked up a flagstone path past a glorious display of multi-colored bougainvillea and hibiscus and into the house. At the rear of an enormous front hall rose a stately stairway guarded by twin mahogany bannisters. Lani peeked to her right and then her left as they approached the steps, but could make out only the parquet floors of the rooms she passed. Her initial impression, however, was of some precious family heirloom, and she thought that Daniel must indeed have been the favorite grandchild to inherit the house.

Daniel paused at the foot of the steps, looking back over his shoulder at the pair who obediently trailed after him. "Please bring in the luggage, Tommy." He fixed Lani with a disapproving stare. "*You* come with me."

"Yes, sir!" she muttered under her breath. When would she ever learn to control her temper? As she followed Daniel up the stairs she swallowed nervously, trying to moisten her throat. Had Daniel's earlier conversation about methods of punishment been meant to be taken seriously?

At the top of the steps they turned into an upper hallway; half-closed doors ran down its length. At the end was Brian's room, which was furnished with bunkbeds and decorated with red, white and blue wallpaper depicting a colonial fife and drum corps. Daniel pulled back the blue quilt on the bottom bed, gently slid Brian in, and removed his shoes. Light from the hallway filtered into the room, revealing shelves containing trucks and ships, jigsaw puzzles and books, blocks and games. Brian would be thrilled when he woke up and explored his new domain.

Lani's bedroom was just across the hall. It was airy

and spacious, with windows on two walls and a sliding glass door to the balcony which would make it especially light and pleasant during the daytime. The predominant color was a dusky rose, which was repeated in the carpet, the striped wallpaper, the tied-back, floor-to-ceiling drapes and the flowered bedspread. A chaise longue and end table sat in one corner; the nighttable, triple dresser and headboard of the double bed were stained a rich, deep brown. At the rear of the room there was a small private bath.

Lani glanced around in silent appreciation of the attractiveness and comfort of the room. At one point in this silent perusal her eyes accidentally met Daniel's, and she hastily looked away. He no longer seemed annoyed with her, but his eyes were glinting in a very unsettling manner, making her remember how very unwise it was to provoke him. She felt her face redden with embarrassment and managed to say stiffly, "It's very nice, Daniel. Thank you."

"I'm happy to know something I do meets with your approval, Lani." He strode out of the room, reappearing a few minutes later accompanied by Tommy and the luggage.

As he left, Tommy gave a casual wave and said he would call Lani the next morning. Somehow, being virtually alone with Daniel in *his* house seemed much more daunting to Lani than being alone with him in her own house. He still held the last of her bags in his hand, but dropped it in the center of the rose-colored rug with a dramatic thud.

"Now. I think you have something to say to me."

Lani checked the impulse to run her palms down the sides of her jeans. She refused to let Daniel see how nervous he made her. "I'm entitled to my opinion about Prescott & Thomas and the way your company has desecrated the islands," she insisted. "Your new hotel . . ."

"You haven't seen my new hotel, or anything else I've done since I came to Hawaii," Daniel reminded her evenly. "Don't you think you should look around before you jump down my throat?"

Of course he was right. He could hardly be blamed for the reckless development of his predecessors, and since she had never inspected any of his personal projects it was unfair to judge them. The shade of her cheeks blended perfectly with the color scheme of the room as she admitted softly, "I suppose. I just . . . well . . . it really upset me, Daniel. Everything is so different now."

"Mostly in Waikiki, princess. Believe me, I understand why you were shocked. I am, too. But the other islands are being developed more carefully." His tone became lightly teasing. "Now don't you think you should apologize for acting like such a wretched little brat?"

In spite of his crushing description of her, Lani knew he wasn't angry anymore, and couldn't resist a saucy reply. "Don't you dare call me a brat," she said. "I'm a woman, not a child."

She was totally unaware of how provocative she looked, with her hands resting on her slender hips and her lower lip thrust out a fraction to give her an enchanting pout. She had straightened up to her full 5'4", her shoulders squared and her back ramrod straight, accentuating the pointed fullness of her breasts. Daniel's eyes traveled up and down the length of her body; his mouth twitched upwards, and he winked at her. "That's one thing we can agree on,

61

princess," he drawled. "Of course, you still have a lot to learn. Lucky for you I'm around to teach you."

Lani felt her cheeks go scarlet, which only amused him further. As he left the room, he was whistling cheerfully to himself, and the tune, she realized in chagrin, was "Thank Heaven for Little Girls."

Chapter Four

Brian came barreling across the hall and into Lani's room the next morning, hurling himself onto her bed and reciting a list of all the "neat" toys he had discovered on his shelves. "Come see what I built!" he urged.

"Okay," Lani mumbled groggily, rubbing her eyes. She pulled on her robe and followed him into his room, yawning as she walked. She had certainly enjoyed more restful nights in her twenty-two years. She had lain awake for hours, trying to fathom Daniel's behavior. In California he had been so consistently impersonal that she felt she could easily keep him at a distance. But from the moment they had landed in Hawaii, he had started to tease her, and those amused smiles of his had a way of sabotaging her composure. Good heavens, if he had taken her in his arms last night, she would probably have woken up in his bed this morning!

There was no longer any point in denying that she found him just as achingly irresistible at twenty-two as she had at fifteen. The thought of it frightened her badly. It was beginning to dawn on her that Daniel had been rather forbearing since Jonathan's death, no doubt because he had promised Jonathan that he would take care of her if anything happened. Perhaps his light teasing was simply intended to lessen the tension between them, but if she took it seriously, and failed to keep a tight rein on her emotions, she would wind up badly hurt.

She really had no alternative, she decided, but to stiffen her defenses and convey to Daniel that while she had agreed to live in his home, she had not granted him the right to interfere in her life. If this arrangement was going to work out at all, it would have to be on a totally impersonal basis. And if her attitude angered him, so be it. She wasn't fifteen anymore, and if she let Daniel get too close to her, he might well accept the invitation she was afraid she would issue. Even his wrath was preferable to that!

Now she raised the woven wood blinds on Brian's windows and paused for several moments to enjoy the view. Several gardeners were hard at work in the back yard, which sloped downward toward the Pacific Ocean. A stone staircase led to the beach, which was partially screened out by the blooms of tropical trees: fiery red tulip trees and royal poinciana, white plumeria, and lavender blue jarcaranda. Half of the yard was terraced to accommodate a tennis court; the other half held an enchanting garden, complete with a central gazebo and occasional tables and chairs hidden away among the shrubs and flowers.

Brian was impatient with Lani's enthusiasm for the colors of the ocean and the gentle roll of the surf. She turned her attention to the airport he had constructed out of maple blocks, lavishly praising how cleverly his airplanes and rocket ships fit into their hangars. Then they started downstairs, with Brian opening each door they passed and dashing into the room beyond. In addition to their own bedrooms, there were two full bathrooms, two rooms furnished as guest bedrooms, and a large, empty room with a tiled floor.

The previous evening Lani had noticed the single door on the other side of the staircase, and assumed it led to the master suite. Brian raced inside before she could stop him, and when Lani cautiously followed she was relieved to find that the child was alone. Beyond the door was a sitting room used as an office, a bedroom furnished in masculine browns and beiges, and a large bathroom. The covers on the king-sized bed were still rumpled, but otherwise the three rooms were quite tidy.

Lani put a stop to Brian's use of the bed as a trampoline and led him downstairs. The dining room was located through an archway near the foot of the steps. Brian ran inside and called out, "I found Daniel!"

Lani followed, trailing her fingers over the softly glowing wood of the inlaid dining room table as she passed it. Daniel was sitting at a circular table in the kitchen beyond. The room was faultlessly modern—a startling contrast to the antique-furnished dining room, with its carved wainscotting and bordered parquet floor.

Daniel sipped his coffee as he glanced up from the newspaper to wish them good morning; he was already dressed for work in a muted gray plaid suit. Brian begged him to go upstairs to look at his airport; while they were gone, Lani poked around the cabinets and located a frying pan to make scrambled eggs in. She was setting Brian's breakfast on the table when he reappeared with Daniel.

"I thought I'd take Brian to the beach today," she said casually. "Maybe Tommy will come along with us." She busied herself with cleaning the counter and washing the dirty pan.

"All right. Just make sure that you're back by 12:30. I arranged . . ."

"Thank you, Daniel. I'm capable of making my own plans." There was no point in delaying her intention of asserting her independence, she had decided.

His disapproving look told her that her assertiveness had annoyed him, perhaps dangerously so. "I'm hiring a full-time housekeeper to replace the woman who used to look after the place part-time for me," he said evenly. "We'll need someone to take care of Brian when you start working. I've scheduled interviews today at 1, 2:30, and 3:30. I'm very busy at the office, Kaiulani, but if a suntan is more important to you than Brian's welfare, I'll come back here to conduct the interviews myself."

Lani was too astonished to speak. Take care of Brian? When she started working? How could he have made such a decision without consulting her first?

Daniel looked across the table at Brian, who had abandoned his preoccupation with breakfast to monitor the conversation. Then he strolled over to Lani, who stood near the sink, and clamped an arm around her shoulder. To Brian, the gesture would look affectionate, but Lani knew better. It might look like a caress, but it was really a warning.

"Cool down, princess," he whispered. Then, in a tone of voice loud enough for Brian to hear, he continued, "Would you like to help Lani pick out someone to take care of you, Brian?"

"I want Lani to take care of me." Lani could tell that her little brother was only inches from a temper tantrum. Her instinctive movement to comfort him was checked by the pressure of Daniel's arm.

"Lani went to school for a long time," he told Brian. "She studied hard so she could find a job she would enjoy."

"She likes taking care of me!" Brian insisted. "I don't want to be left with some mean old lady."

"They're all young and pretty and nice," Daniel teased. "And most of the day you'll be in camp, with other children your own age. You and Lani can have a vacation for a few weeks, but then she's going to work and you're going to camp. You can swim and play games, and even learn to ride a horse. How does that sound?"

Brian stared at Daniel for several long seconds, his lower lip quivering slightly. To Lani's amazement, instead of running from the room in tears he asked slyly, "Can I have cowboy boots?"

"Sure, if they make them in your size. I think they teach you to snorkel, too."

"I tried that in Christopher's pool. It was neat!" Brian exclaimed.

"Good. Now that that's settled, go upstairs and change into some clean clothes. I want to talk to your sister for a while."

Brian ran out of the room, still grinning at the prospect of camp. Lani pulled away from Daniel. How on earth was she going to assert her independence when she felt like flinging herself into his arms every time he touched her? With great effort, she regrouped her defenses and told him firmly, "I'm not taking a job. Hire a housekeeper if you want to, and by all means send Brian to camp if he wants to go, but my place is here. I'm not having him come home every day to some stranger."

"You've been his mother since you were sixteen years old. It's time you started living your own life. You'll be working for the hotel . . ."

"I'll find my own job!" Lani fumed, glaring at him. "Stop trying to run me!"

A sharp look accompanied Daniel's ominous silence, causing Lani to color defensively and lower her eyes to the floor. She wasn't going to apologize for interrupting him—not when his highhanded decision had goaded her into the very reaction he found so offensive. But when he finally replied, his tone was measured. "You're really leaning on me, princess. Remember what happened seven years ago."

Her blue eyes flashing, Lani jerked her head up to confront him. "Is that supposed to be the ultimate threat? That if I don't toe the mark, you'll kiss me? It just might work, Daniel. It was a pretty bruising experience, in more ways than one!"

"No, damn you!" he exploded. "I meant that if you keep pushing me, I'm going to push back. Being even-tempered isn't one of my strong points, especially where you're concerned."

He stalked over to the coffee maker, poured himself a generous mugful of coffee, and stirred in a small amount of sugar. As he leaned against the counter and sipped it, Lani had the feeling that he was more interested in controlling his anger than in quenching his thirst.

His next nonchalant comment left her stunned. "When I get around to making love to you, princess, you'll enjoy it," he said. "So much so that you won't want me to stop, I promise you." And then he grinned at her horrified reaction.

When he got around to making love to her? What was that supposed to mean? It sounded to Lani as if Daniel meant to add her to the list of women he planned to favor with his attentions, and she could never cope with that. Even his mild flirtatiousness was impossible for her to handle. Obviously he was simply teasing her again, trying to throw her off balance.

The whole topic was much too dangerous, so she switched back to the question of whether or not she should take a job. "If I go to work, it might have a bad effect on Brian," she suggested warily.

"Both of us love Brian, but he's six years old now and there's no reason he can't spend a few hours a day with a sitter. By all means take the next three weeks to help him settle in, but after the Fourth of July holiday he starts camp and you start work. You've sacrificed enough of your life, Lani. I won't let it continue."

Perhaps he had a point, Lani admitted. She knew she would enjoy the challenge of a job, not to mention the opportunity to meet new people and gain some independence. But even if she agreed to go to work, she would never accept employment in one of Prescott & Thomas's hotels.

There was no reason to antagonize Daniel by saying so, however. She merely nodded and murmured, "I'd prefer to find my own job. Please, Daniel."

"I'm not giving you a choice. If you insist on taking a job other than the one I've got in mind, I'll simply talk to your employer and get you fired."

He probably had the connections to do exactly that! "That's not fair," Lani muttered, as much to herself as to Daniel.

"Maybe not," he answered, "but I've come up with the perfect job for you, and unless I miss my guess, even you'll agree."

"Really!" Her interest was piqued, there was no point in denying it.

"Really. You're going to be the VIP tour guide for the Maunalua Bay. It's not your average tourist haunt, princess. We're after two types of business. The first is the vacationer who demands elegance and quiet but chooses Oahu over one of the neighbor islands because the excitement of Honolulu is readily available if he wants it. The second—our real bread and butter—will be small conventions and business meetings. It won't be easy to snare that business away from other hotels. We aim to give the potential customer a few extras in addition to the usual free ride. When a businessman comes here to look us over, I want someone special to show him a good time. The same thing goes for other VIP types—heads of state, royalty, that sort of thing. You're perfect for the job: a native-born Hawaiian, young, beautiful, and multi-lingual. And," he added seductively, "you could arrange most of your sightseeing for the morning and early afternoon. You could be home before Brian."

Lani's once-firm opinion as to the wickedness of Prescott & Thomas began to crumble as Daniel told her about the position he had in mind for her. She loved her home state and she loved being with interesting people. Showing the first to the second would be sheer bliss. She would be able to utilize her considerable linguistic ability, and best of all, she would be home to greet Brian most of the time. Her objection was really only a token one. "I'd want to see the hotel first. To see if I approve of what you've done."

"You've got it, princess. I'll call the manager and

70

make an appointment. Her name is Michiko Hansen. How about tomorrow at ten?"

Lani impatiently quelled the stab of disappointment she felt because Daniel wouldn't be performing the task himself. Why should it matter to her? After all, hadn't she decided that an impersonal relationship was best? She forced herself to smile, saying, "Sure, that's fine," just as Brian reappeared.

"Are you guys still talking?" he asked in exasperation. "I thought Daniel had to go to work."

"I do." Daniel ruffled the boy's hair. "Your big sister was giving me a hard time." The child seemed to find this inordinately funny, and giggled loudly as Daniel turned his attention back to Lani.

"Will you take care of hiring somebody, or do I have to come home?"

Lani didn't miss the amused sparkle in his eye, and couldn't resist answering pertly, "Won't you want to speak to the applicants yourself? Are you sure you trust me to make an acceptable choice?"

Daniel chose to take the questions literally. "No and yes. I'd say you're a good judge of character, princess, except in one case."

"Which is?"

"Me, of course," he replied, and added teasingly, "Some day you'll realize that intelligence, money, and good looks aren't my only assets."

Lani could have kicked herself for walking blindly into the trap he had set. "Right," she shot back. "There's also your humility and your policy of not interfering in other people's lives."

Daniel simply winked at Brian and asked, "See what I mean? She's giving me a hard time again." He picked up a leather attache case from the counter, pausing only long enough to reel off the salary he wanted her to offer, along with suggested working hours and days off. A vague gesture to his left indicated the location of the bedroom and bath to be occupied by the housekeeper.

Brian immediately bolted away to examine this area of the house, with Lani following at a more moderate pace. After satisfying herself that the spacious room was immaculate, she decided to make a brief inspection of the rest of the house. The focal point of the living room was a beautiful marble fireplace, flanked by cherry pillars. The room was furnished with early American antiques that Lani assumed were originals and not copies, just like the impressionist paintings which hung beneath the plaster cornices that hugged the ceiling. The first floor also contained a library, an informal back parlor, and a powder room, with an airy, screened porch to the rear.

As Lani went upstairs to dress, she admitted to herself that she couldn't fault her stepbrother's taste in furnishings. The house was beautiful. She had just stepped out of the shower when the phone rang, and she hurriedly grabbed a towel and ran back into the bedroom to pick it up.

"Hi, Lani." Tommy Prescott sounded cheerful this morning. "Can I take you and the kid to the beach today?"

"I was planning on it," Lani answered with a laugh, finding the interruption a welcome one. "But we have to be back by 12:30. Daniel wants me to hire a housekeeper today. He's got the whole thing organized; three applicants are coming in for interviews."

"Typical Prescott efficiency. I'll be there in twenty minutes, so be ready."

Lani replied teasingly that Tommy as well as Daniel had inherited a penchant for efficiency and hung up.

After calling across the hall to Brian to change into a bathing suit, she slipped on her own one-piece blue suit and a matching terry cover-up. The halter-necked suit plunged to the waist in back and was cut high on the leg to accentuate her considerable assets.

While she and Brian were waiting for Tommy to arrive they entertained themselves by inspecting the family portraits in the hall. Daniel's mother, Laura, had been a dusky-skinned beauty, and even his grandmother, the formidable Victoria, had been attractive in spite of her stern appearance. But most of all Lani was captivated by the Hawaiian princess who had brought wealth and influence into the Prescott clan. In her ornate European-style wedding gown she seemed only a child, though a stunningly lovely one. "I want my babysitter to look like her," Brian announced.

Tommy drove them to Waikiki Beach, sliding the Porsche into a parking space too small for most cars. Although the beach was more crowded than it had been when Lani was a child, she could hardly complain. On any summer weekend her favorite beach in San Diego was a mass of human bodies, and this was no worse. Brian ran off toward the water and quickly made friends with a group of children who were building an elaborate sand castle near the shoreline; Tommy excused himself to rent a surfboard and headed toward the waves with it.

Lani was content to sunbathe, leaning languidly back in the canvas chair Tommy had thoughtfully brought along for her. Later on, she took Brian for a swim and then sat crosslegged at the shoreline, helping the children with their castle.

Tommy returned just as she and Brian were walking back from the refreshment stand, carrying a trio of soft drinks. The child lost no time in scampering back to his new friends.

"Your timing is perfect," Lani told Tommy, handing him a cola. "How was the surfing?"

"Good for beginners. Boring for me."

False modesty certainly wasn't a Prescott vice, Lani thought to herself as she suppressed a smile. She and Tommy sat down on their towels to talk, Lani mentioning the job she would be starting in July and asking Tommy about his own plans for the summer.

"It's really my last shot at freedom," he said. "Once I start law school, I'll be working as an intern in the legal department. But this summer I'll fill in wherever Michi—the manager—needs someone. There isn't much I haven't done, including putting on a grass skirt and impersonating a Tahitian dancer," he grinned. "I start Monday."

"I'm going to miss you." Lani knew it was the truth. Tommy provided undemanding, pleasant company, and she found his irreverent attitude toward his high-and-mighty older cousin especially refreshing.

"Maybe we can see each other on my days off. Not my nights off, though," he added ruefully. "Daniel's pretty protective of you, Lani. Maybe you don't get along, but last night he laid down the ground rules. I don't ask you out until we know each other better. I'm not supposed to rush you."

Lani was surprised that she felt rather grateful to Daniel for that. After all, it wasn't as though he had forbidden his cousin to date her—he had simply told Tommy to wait. It was obvious that Tommy, although only her own age, was vastly more experienced than she was.

"Anyway," he went on with a shrug, "if I don't do what Daniel says, I'm going to find myself on the next plane off the island. And I like it here. It's where the action is."

"Would he really do it? Send you to Molokai, I mean?" Lani asked.

Now Tommy began to laugh. "Kona, more likely. Have you figured out what was going on last night?"

"I think so. You took that route because you knew how I'd react. You wanted to get in a few licks at Daniel and you used me to do it. Is that right?"

Tommy's nod confirmed the accuracy of her guess. "I couldn't resist, Lani. I hope it didn't get you into trouble."

"Not really." Lani had no intention of repeating her conversation with Daniel, especially given the embarrassing content of it.

"I didn't think it would, because you're part of the family, and Daniel's pretty tolerant when it comes to people he cares about. He delivered a few choice words last night, then started to laugh. He takes things from me and my sister that he'd never put up with from anyone else."

Did Lani fit into that category? The thought that Daniel might have some affection for her was enough to suffuse her body with a dangerous warmth that owed nothing to the tropical sun. How was she to fight such feelings? Coolness wasn't keeping Daniel at a distance. Perhaps she should simply follow his lead, and adopt a light, teasing manner similar to his own.

She eased herself onto her stomach and began to question Tommy about his family, a much safer topic of conversation than Daniel's feelings for her. She learned that his sister Hope had just completed her senior year in high school as a foreign exchange student in Japan. Tommy's parents were currently in the Far East to pick her up; all three would continue with a combined vacation/business trip. Both Japan and Hong Kong were potentially lucrative markets, not only for tourism but for shipping, agriculture, and real estate as well.

Tommy dropped them off just in time for Lani to shower the sand from her hair and change into a white terry shirtwaist with maroon and navy trim. All three job applicants were excellent, but both she and Brian preferred the final one. Linda Wong was twenty years old, the oldest of six children, and quite accustomed to taking care of her younger siblings, including a boy of just Brian's age whom she tentatively suggested would be a suitable playmate for Brian if she got the job. She spoke to Brian with the naturalness and affection of an experienced mother, and after she left, Lani immediately phoned several of the people listed as references. Their recommendations were glowing indeed, and Lani wasted no time in phoning the agency to inform them of her decision.

When she called Linda, the girl seemed so thrilled to get the job that Lani questioned her as to why a young woman with her obvious intelligence and ambition would be willing to tie herself down as a housekeeper. Linda's reply was refreshingly candid. She was a part-time student, and it would take her several more years to finish college, she explained. After she graduated, she intended to work for an established company offering good opportunities for advancement. The competition for such positions was fierce. Originally she had been looking for an office job, but when the agency mentioned her prospective employer she quickly changed her mind. She told Lani that she hoped Mr. Reid would be impressed enough to give her a chance with Prescott & Thomas when she graduated, and Lani replied that she was certain he would give the matter his consideration.

They agreed that Linda would begin work a week from Monday in order to give Brian a few weeks to get used to being with her. Lani heard the front door open just as she was making final arrangements with Linda and Daniel walked in. His glance flickered over her and then to Brian, who was still in his bathing suit. "Go put on a shirt and pants. We're going out to dinner," he said to the child.

Brian dashed out of the kitchen at his usual breakneck pace, just as Lani was hanging up the phone. "Sounds like you hired someone," Daniel commented.

Lani told him about Linda Wong's background, stressing that the girl seemed reliable and fond of children. "She wants to work for Prescott & Thomas when she graduates," she added. "She's determined to impress you into offering her a job."

"Dusting my desk?" Daniel asked dryly.

"She's a business major. You *will* consider it when the time comes, won't you, Daniel?" Lani knew she would feel horribly guilty if Linda put in three or four years as a housekeeper when there was no chance of eventual employment with Prescott & Thomas.

"I'll make her Vice President for Maintenance," he said solemnly. "When does the future executive start?"

Lani had to giggle at the joke. "A week from Monday. About dinner . . . I would have cooked something, but there's not much in the house and without a car . . ."

"Be patient, princess," Daniel replied in a teasing voice. "I'm a busy man. We'll pick out a car this weekend."

"I wasn't hinting!"

"You can't take corporate presidents on the bus, Miss Douglas. You'll need a comfortable car. Do you like the one I drive?"

"Such a big car?" Lani asked, feigning dismay. "Can't I have two? A neat little sportscar for me, and a big limousine for the VIP's?"

He didn't seem to realize that she was kidding. "I don't like the thought of you driving around in a sportscar. Big cars are safer."

"Besides, you can charge it off to the business, right, Mr. Reid?" She gave him a big grin.

"That's right, princess," he replied. "Just like tonight's dinner. We've had too many complaints about the food and service in one of the hotels we acquired last year. It's time I checked it out."

Lani's sense of humor was too well developed to suppress a gurgle of laughter. "Wonderful!" she giggled. "Our first night in Hawaii, and where do you take us to dinner? A dreadful restaurant with even worse service."

She was astonished to see his face redden under his dark tan. "I didn't think of that, Lani. I'm sorry. We'll do it another night."

"Oh, no!" Lani answered with a mocking shake of her head. "I wouldn't miss your third-rate restaurant for the world!" It was intensely gratifying to her that not every outpost of Daniel's empire was a sanctuary of gracious perfection.

"It's not third-rate," he said stiffly, "just not up to our usual standards."

Lani had never seen her stepbrother quite so put out, but mercifully Brian chose that moment to reappear. "We're going to one of your big brother's restaurants for dinner," Lani told him in a low, conspiratorial voice. "We're going to be spies. We test the food, and see if the waiter does a good job, and then make a secret report."

Brian was delighted with the idea, so much so that his

behavior at the restaurant was a good deal more restrained then usual.

"I'm amazed that no one's recognized you," Lani commented to Daniel after they had ordered their meals. "I thought Daniel Prescott Reid was famous throughout the entire North Pacific region."

Daniel had long ago recovered from his previous chagrin, and now he lazed back in his chair and regarded Lani through half-lidded, amused gray eyes. "Naturally. The South Pacific too. But people recognize the name more readily than the face." He reached out a long arm to take a package of salted bread sticks from a wicker basket on the table, opened it, and popped one into his mouth. "Now if I had come in with Michi or Elizabeth, it might be different. People expect to see me with a beautiful woman in tow. But this," he gestured toward Brian, "is a very domestic scene."

Lani shot him a dirty look. "Gee Daniel, thanks for the compliment!" Michi, she told herself, must be Michiko Hansen, the general manager of the Maunalua Bay Hotel. But who was Elizabeth?

He only smiled and ate another bread stick. "You're in a class by yourself, princess," he informed her.

Then the waiter appeared with their salads, and Lani gratefully turned her attention to her meal. The plate, she noticed, was still warm, as if it had recently come out of the dishwasher, and the dressing had a slight off taste.

At first Daniel expressed his displeasure with his dinner with a series of acerbic judgments, but eventually he succumbed to Lani and Brian's lighthearted mood and began to joke about the restaurant's flaws. Although the quality of the ingredients was excellent, the preparation was mundane and the service just clumsy enough to be an annoyance. As Daniel relaxed, he became increasingly affable—almost human, Lani decided.

His apparent good mood vanished the moment he excused himself to approach the restaurant's manager. Lani knew that stern look—she had been on the receiving end far too often. She felt sorry for the man as he gave them a guided tour of the kitchen. His face was dewy with discomfort, and turned pink when Daniel began to poke through cabinets and drawers. The kitchen looked clean enough to Lani's untrained eye, but Daniel had pulled out a small notepad and was jotting down deficiencies as the staff silently looked on.

"What are you going to do?" Lani asked as they walked to the car.

"Call the hotel's general manager. Follow it up with a written report. Recommend the replacement of the restaurant manager and the head chef."

"No warning?" Such abrupt action seemed rather heartless to Lani.

"They've had complaints, and that's warning enough. No one likes to fire people, Lani, but if you run a business, sometimes it's necessary."

"I'm glad I don't have your job," she admitted. She was beginning to understand just what kinds of pressures Daniel lived with, and just how hard he worked.

Before returning home, they drove around the Waikiki area, and Lani was amazed at the number of tourists who strolled through the streets, dressed in everything from jeans to colorfully printed aloha fashions. Daniel pointed out the other two Prescott & Thomas hotels, both of which were over a decade old. Although she was pleased to learn that the company planned renovations and additional landscaping, she would have preferred that half the hotels on the strip be torn down and replaced by palm trees and bougainvillea. Noise, traffic, concrete, and crowds were not her idea of a tropical paradise.

Since Daniel was already much too familiar with her point of view, she refrained from restating it. Somehow, she told herself, the two of them had managed to spend an entire evening together without exchanging bitter words or angry looks. On the contrary, the last few hours had been all too pleasant. Maybe she was an utter fool, but at that moment, she had no desire to renew hostilities.

Chapter Five

Tommy Prescott called the next morning at nine o'clock.

"I've got my marching orders," he announced. "I'm supposed to pick you up at a quarter of ten and run you up to the hotel, then take the kid off your hands while Michi gives you the grand tour."

Lani had planned to take the bus, and ordinarily she would have welcomed Tommy's offer of a ride. Under the circumstances she rejected it, irritated with Daniel for making arrangements without consulting her. "Really?" she asked icily.

Laughter rang through the receiver. "He didn't tell you, huh? Don't be too hard on him. Giving orders comes naturally to Daniel."

Lani smoldered with anger. "He can give them to someone else, then! I'll get there on my own."

"No, you won't. You'll go with me!" Typical Prescott

arrogance, Lani thought rebelliously. In ten years, Tommy would be every bit as overbearing as Daniel.

Nonetheless, at the moment he was only twenty-two, and when she maintained a stony silence, his self-confidence seemed to desert him. "C'mon, Lani. Let me take you. I'm liable to wind up washing dishes in Kona if you don't."

"He wouldn't take it out on you. I thought he was so *tolerant* of his family," she said in a saccharine tone.

"Ouch!" Lani could imagine the accompanying wince. "Have a heart, Lani. He *will* take it out on me." There was an awkward pause. "Uh, look. I guess . . . that is, I was supposed to ask if you wanted to go to the beach, and when you told me you'd be at the hotel, I was supposed to offer to take you up there. How about it?"

Recalling Tommy's devious baiting of his cousin during the drive home from the airport, Lani began to suspect that his ingenuous explanation was more than a little self-serving. "You did it on purpose, didn't you? You told me that Daniel had given you orders because you wanted me to be angry with him."

"Okay, I admit it. I'm still smarting over his dictum about not taking you out. Typical Prescott highhandedness. If I weren't one of us," Tommy added good-naturedly, "I'd resent it like mad."

His light-hearted confession was so irresistible that Lani found it impossible to remain annoyed with him. After all, she could hardly blame him for taking a few swipes at his cousin when she herself had done so on many occasions during the last seven years. She told him to come by in forty-five minutes, and added that she would pack a flight bag with Brian's suit and towel in case they decided to go to the beach again.

As for Daniel's behavior, she supposed she should

bristle, but after last night she couldn't bring herself to object. In fact, it would provide a convenient excuse to tease him about his habit of failing to consult her about plans made on her behalf. And Lani had discovered that she enjoyed teasing Daniel. She liked the warm look that came into his eyes, and the way he smiled at her.

The Maunalua Bay Hotel was located "kokohead"— toward Koko Head Crater, to the east of the Kahala District. The access road from the highway cut through a manicured golf course situated adjacent to the hotel itself. The main building was designed in a gentle arc which mimicked the curve of the shoreline, while a two-story extension curved away from the fifteen-story tower to make an S-shaped complex. Trees and flowering shrubs softened the modern facade of the hotel.

Tommy pulled the car up to the front entrance to drop Lani off. Like many hotels in Hawaii, the Maunalua Bay had no front doors, a feature designed to take advantage of the natural air conditioning provided by the ocean breeze. Lani gave Brian a hug and kiss good-bye and walked through a high archway into the lobby. It was an enormous, high-ceilinged room with a central crystal chandelier, a dark tiled floor and an oval carpet on which groups of chairs and sofas were placed. Numerous plants blended with an earth-tone color scheme to give the lobby a natural, restful feeling.

Lani stopped at the registration desk to ask directions to the manager's office, then proceeded past a bank of elevators and into a hall where a discreet sign and arrow indicated the location of the administrative offices. She knocked lightly at the door labeled "General Manager."

A musical female voice replied, "Come in!"

Lani had no preconceived mental image of Michi Hansen, but if she had, it would never have measured up to the exquisite creature who confronted her. She appeared to be in her mid-30s, at the height of her beauty. Even in her spiked heels she was several inches smaller than Lani's own 5'4". Her dark hair was a shimmering, silky cap; her dark, almond-shaped eyes were warm with welcome. Her perfectly proportioned, curvaceous body was clad in an elegant beige silk skirtsuit, the jacket belted with black leather. Lani wished that she had worn something more formal than her blue and white dotted swiss sundress. With its blouson top and slender straps it was quite charming, but definitely not in the same sophisticated league as the older woman's attire.

Michi Hansen crossed the room with businesslike strides that seemed wholly out of place given her delicate appearance. As she extended her right hand, Lani noticed the filigreed gold band on her left ring finger. "I'm very happy to meet you at last," the manager said with a smile. "Or perhaps I should say, *"Hagime-mashite do-zo yoroshi-ku."* She had repeated her welcome in Japanese.

Lani answered in the same language, complimenting her on the beauty of the hotel.

"I can't take the credit, I'm afraid," Michi said, switching back to English. "It was designed by a brilliant young architect, a local boy Daniel discovered. As you can see, the result justifies Daniel's confidence in him."

Lani nodded, expecting that the manager's comment was a prelude to the upcoming tour, but instead of leading Lani back to the lobby, Michi Hansen invited her to sit down on the sofa and offered her some coffee.

"No, thank you." Lani watched as Michi poured

some coffee from the coffee maker on her credenza into a bone china cup, then seated herself in an armchair next to the sofa.

"Your Japanese is excellent. Where did you learn to speak it so well?" the manager asked.

"When I was growing up in Hawaii, my best friend was Japanese," Lani explained. "I spent as much time at her house as at my own, and I gradually picked it up. Even though we moved to California when I was ten, it stayed with me, because when I started taking the language in college, it all came back. Foreign languages are easy for me—I speak French and Spanish too, plus some Hawaiian, of course."

"I can see you'll be a great asset to us, Lani." Michi Hansen's smile was beguiling. "I confess I've been dying to meet you. Daniel has spoken of you so often."

"Probably all of it bad," Lani blurted out, then blushed furiously. "What I mean," she added awkwardly, "is that we don't always get along very well. I guess it's mostly my fault."

"Not at all," was the smooth reply. "Daniel is well aware that he shares in the blame. He has difficulty in controlling his temper where you're concerned. I think you'll notice a great improvement now that you're here in Hawaii."

Michi's gaze was so direct and intent that Lani felt pressured to make a revealing reply, something she had no intention of doing. The manager might look as ethereal and delicate as a white ginger blossom, but inside, Lani suspected, she was as tough as the fibrous leaves of that same plant. Since bluntness seemed to be the order of the day, she asked Michi, "How long have you known my stepbrother?"

"Six years. My husband Keith was the assistant manager of a hotel on the Big Island when Daniel recruited him for a similar position at one of Prescott & Thomas's Waikiki hotels. The three of us became good friends almost immediately. As our daughter Sarah grew up, I found myself spending more and more time helping Keith. We became a team, and were promoted to co-managers two years later. Last year, when the company approved plans for the Maunalua Bay, Daniel told us he wanted us to manage it." Michi's voice and eyes softened. "Keith was killed in an automobile accident ten months ago. Daniel persuaded me that I would be capable of managing the hotel without my husband. He's been wonderful since Keith died. I couldn't ask for a finer employer or a better friend."

"I'm sorry," Lani murmured huskily. "I know what it's like . . ." Unshed tears forced her to stop, as a kaleidoscope of mental images swirled in her mind: Anne, pale with the effort of childbirth; Jonathan, in the hospital after his second heart attack; herself, at two funerals. She had lost so very much. At the same time, she felt a stab of pain that puzzled her until she realized that it had nothing to do with her parents' deaths. It stemmed from the fact that Daniel had taken care of Michi Hansen when she needed someone to lean on. Lani had been his stepsister for fourteen years, yet never had he treated her with such kindness and gentleness. Could she possibly be jealous of Michi?

She wondered if Daniel was in love with the beautiful hotel manager. Michi Hansen seemed to have everything he could require in a woman: warmth, charm, intelligence, independence, and an ability to share in his work. And she was beautiful beyond words. It was obvious that she had not yet recovered from her husband's death, but when she did, would Daniel ask her to marry him?

"I've upset you." The soft, contrite words broke into

Lani's speculations. "It was thoughtless of me to mention Keith when your loss is so much more recent. Can I get you a glass of water or show you to the ladies' room?"

Lani shook her head and reached into her purse for a tissue. Although her eyes were dry, the pretense of dabbing at them gave her a few moments to regain her composure. She managed a brief smile. "I'm fine, really. I'd love to see the hotel."

Michi glanced at the diamond and gold watch on her wrist. "Good. Daniel should be here any minute. Let's wait for him in the lobby."

"Daniel?" The word came out in a squeak. Daniel hadn't said anything about coming today. In fact, he had given her quite the opposite impression.

"Of course," was the amused reply. "You could hardly expect your stepbrother to permit anyone else to show you around the hotel. He's as proud as a brand-new father, but in this case," Michi joked, "the baby was a rather large one."

They entered the lobby to find Daniel talking to a uniformed security guard, his long strides bringing him to their side a moment later. Michi held out both hands to him as he approached and he took them in his own, bending his head to brush her mouth.

"How are you and Lani getting along?" he murmured.

Michi gently took her hands from his and backed away several steps. "Very well. We've been talking about you."

The statement seemed to remind Daniel of Lani's presence. "Telling Michi all your complaints about me, no doubt," he said with a teasing smile.

"That would take more than fifteen minutes," Lani

retorted with a laugh, "starting with your call to Tommy this morning."

Daniel looked rather sheepish as he draped an arm over her shoulder. "Later, princess. Right now I want to show you around."

Lani allowed him to escort her across the lobby to the hotel shops. In addition to the usual sundries shop there were several clothing stores, a florist, a fine jewelry store, an art gallery, and a gift shop featuring exquisite collectors' items made of a variety of precious materials. Lani's automatic estimate of the prices in these stores told her a good deal about the affluence of the clientele.

They proceeded to the top floor, which housed one of the hotel's two restaurants as well as a large nightclub/bar. The floor-to-ceiling picture windows in both provided a dazzling view of the Koolau mountain range to one side and the Pacific Ocean to the other. Daniel explained that the restaurant was open to the public only for dinner; the nightclub was used for the hotel's twice-nightly shows.

Michi opened up several of the guest suites and rooms on the floor below. Neither the two room suites nor the individual rooms were as large as Lani had expected, although she admitted to herself that the earth-tone color scheme was charming. Each room had a private balcony overlooking either the ocean or the golf course.

They rode back downstairs and left the building through the rear of the lobby. To her right, Lani noticed the parking garage; Daniel explained that most of the structure had been built underground, so as not to obstruct the view. They walked under a covered walkway past a pond where brightly colored tropical fish swam languidly. The hotel's other restaurant, the Bay Terrace, was housed on the second floor of a separate building adjacent to the fish pond.

After a brief inspection of the conference facilities on the first floor, they returned to the restaurant. Because of the slope of the hill on which the hotel sat, the dining room was level with the main lobby. In spite of the pristine white linen, silver-plated flatware and china vases filled with scarlet anthurium flowers, the atmosphere here was less formal than in the Koolau Room on the fifteenth floor. Many of the diners were attired only in cover-ups and sandals.

The hotel's oval-shaped pool was located to the other side of the Bay Terrace, surrounded by a concrete patio. Recumbent sun worshippers occupied every available lounge chair; a nearby stand offered snacks, sandwiches, and soft drinks, while the poolside bar did a brisk business in cocktails and exotic drinks. Beyond the patio were a wide strip of lawn and a narrower expanse of sand, markers on each side indicating a coral-free area for swimming.

In back of the pool there was a row of tall trees screening out a delightful garden of profusely blooming tropical plants. Although any guest could enjoy a stroll along the paths that twisted through the shrubbery, the garden functioned as an exotic front yard for the two-story extension Lani had noticed from the highway.

"These are the hotel's most expensive suites," Daniel remarked, and glanced at Michi. "Can we get into one?"

"At the far end, Daniel." She opened the door with a pass key, revealing a miniature apartment complete with sitting room, bath and dining area downstairs, and two bedrooms and two bathrooms upstairs. Lani surveyed the luxurious fittings, including a fully stocked bar, bowls of fresh flowers and fruit, plush carpeting, and expensive furnishings. "How much do you charge for this?" she gasped.

Daniel named a nightly figure higher than what some people earned in a month. "But most of our suites are less expensive. We have a total of twenty-six, most of them with only two rooms."

Their final stop was the ground floor, which housed additional conference and housekeeping facilities.

"Would you like to have lunch, Michi?" Daniel asked as they rode the elevator back up to the lobby.

"I can't." The petite brunette glanced at her watch. "I've scheduled a meeting with the convention manager in ten minutes. May I take a raincheck, Daniel?"

"Don't even mention that word!" he admonished, sliding his arm around Michi's shoulder as his mouth briefly covered hers. "They come for the sunshine, remember?"

Michi and Daniel began to discuss the upcoming meeting, and Lani, feeling uncomfortably ignorant about the topic, slipped away from them toward the hotel stores. She spent several minutes browsing in the art gallery, then looked through the season's newest swimsuits. She was examining a provocative wisp of black nylon when two hands came down squarely on her shoulders, causing her to start and swing around.

"Why don't you try it on?" Daniel asked teasingly.

Lani quickly moved away. "You startled me," she said breathlessly.

"You're lucky that's all I did, Miss Douglas. Why did you disappear like that? I've been looking for you for the last ten minutes."

91

"You and Michi were talking business, and I felt . . . in the way," Lani admitted. "I don't know anything about running a hotel."

"Which is why I'm taking you to lunch." He took her arm to lead her toward the lobby.

Lani refused to budge. It was the perfect time to introduce Daniel to the custom of issuing invitations instead of orders, and she took full advantage of it. "First Tommy, now lunch. Don't you ever get bored with bossing me around?" She slanted him a beguiling look from under her lashes.

"What about Tommy?" he asked innocently.

As if he didn't know! "You *ordered* him to pick me up this morning. You should have asked me whether I wanted to go with him."

"Why wouldn't you want to? Did he try to seduce you in the bucket seat of his Porsche yesterday?" A smile was pulling at the corners of his mouth.

"Very funny! And that's another thing, Mr. Reid. Since when do you tell me who I can date? If I want to go out with Tommy . . ."

"I told *him,* not you. And you should thank me for it. I wouldn't trust my cousin with any female over the age of sixteen." By now Daniel was grinning openly. "Just looking out for your virtue, princess."

"You're impossible!" Lani threw up her hands in exasperation and started to walk away, but succeeded in taking only two steps before Daniel's hands wrapped themselves around her waist and pulled her back against him.

The contact made her heart beat doubletime, and when he bent his head to whisper in her ear, the warm breath on her cheek seemed to flame through her whole body. "Flirting with me, princess?" he asked softly.

Of course she had been, but she would never admit to it. "Let me go!" she hissed.

"Promise not to run away?"

At that moment Lani would have agreed to anything in order to end the dizzying sensations his hard body was causing in hers. She should have known better than to play such games with Daniel. He must feel the way she was trembling, held so close against him. "I won't run away," she quickly agreed.

He released her, turning her in his arms and kissing her gently on the forehead. "Sorry about this morning, princess. I planned to pick you up myself, and when I got tied up I called Tommy, who obviously couldn't resist the opportunity to get in a few digs. Next time," he added easily, "I'll call you first. Now how about lunch?"

"Yes . . . sure," Lani murmured, rather stunned by his kiss and subsequent apology. He wouldn't act so gentle unless he really cared about her, would he? Secretly pleased by the thought, she allowed herself to be led over to the Bay Terrace.

"Good afternoon, Mr. Reid. It's nice to see you here again. Where would you like to sit?" It was obvious to Lani that the hostess's admiring look owed as much to Daniel's masculine appeal as to his position as a top executive with Prescott & Thomas.

"I think perhaps the lady would like to decide. Lani? Would you like to watch the ocean or the fish pond?"

"The fish pond," Lani said, smiling up at Daniel as a reward for consulting her.

He glanced at the menu, then suggested that they order the mahimahi, a local fish which the chef prepared in a white wine sauce. Lani readily agreed. A moment later, he asked briskly, "What do you think of the hotel?"

Lani was surprised by the shuttered wariness on his face, almost like a suitor anticipating a rejection from his beloved. But of course she was being fanciful. Her opinion was of no importance to Daniel except in a business sense. He wanted her services as a guide.

Even so, Lani thought the hotel was a showplace. But since she and Daniel had been getting along so well, she thought it safe to tease him slightly. "I preferred the unspoiled beach, but I suppose if you're going to destroy the natural beauty of Hawaii, a hotel like this is better than some slipshod tourist trap. Of course," she added airily, "you have to be a millionaire to stay here."

"One of your typical exaggerations," he answered in a crushing tone. "You're appalled by the quality of some of the construction over in Waikiki, but you want a hotel to be beautiful and exclusive *and* offer moderately priced accommodations. You can't have it both ways. A place like the Maunalua Bay costs a fortune to build and maintain. Prescott & Thomas expects to make a profit from its ventures, and we charge accordingly. Even so, you can rent a double room here for only twenty or thirty dollars more than in a comparable Waikiki hotel. So we come back to my original question. Given that I've desecrated eight hundred feet of pristine beachfront property, do you approve of the hotel?"

Lani felt as though Daniel had just tossed her into his office paper shredder. She stared across at him, a totally stricken look on her face.

"Oh, no, you were kidding me, weren't you?" The words were contrite, and Daniel didn't wait for an answer. "I'm so used to the way you've always gibed at me . . . I'm sorry, honey."

"Your hotel is beautiful, Daniel," Lani answered

softly. "Everything is perfect—the architecture, the landscaping, the decoration. Even a dyed-in-the-wool environmentalist couldn't object." Then taking in the self-satisfied expression on his face, she risked adding, "The only thing you're missing is the dolphins."

"The Kahala Hilton beat us to it," he grinned. "One doesn't want to be too imitative."

The waiter appeared to take their orders for lunch, and while they waited for their meals, Daniel outlined the staffing requirements of the three-hundred-fourteen-room hotel, which employed well over a hundred people in a dozen different departments. As General Manager, Michi Hansen oversaw every aspect of the hotel's operation. Lani felt like an incompetent child in comparison to the sophisticated, highly capable widow.

During lunch, Daniel continued with a description of some of the problems and challenges Prescott & Thomas had encountered in designing and building the Maunalua Bay. By the time Lani attacked her dessert, a sinfully fattening concoction of tropical fruit wrapped in crepes and garnished with chocolate curls and whipped cream, she was almost spellbound with admiration for Daniel. If his other resorts were as lovely as this hotel, she looked forward to seeing them.

"By the way," Daniel said casually as Lani giggled over an amusing anecdote, "Michi was telling me that my cousin Richard called her this morning. He's in Japan, with his wife and daughter."

"I know," Lani said. "Tommy told me about it."

"His daughter's Japanese family gave a farewell reception for the Prescotts, and Richard struck up a conversation with a fellow named Isamu Mayakawa. Does the name ring a bell?"

"Mayakawa? You mean Mayakawa Electronics?" Lani asked with interest.

"Very good. He's bringing his wife and daughter to Hawaii for a vacation next week. Richard talked him into cancelling his Waikiki reservations and staying with us; he seemed to think Mayakawa could be persuaded to schedule his next worldwide sales conference with us."

Lani set her fork on the dessert plate, feeling a familiar pressure build up along her jaw and neck. How could she have been so stupid as to think that Daniel had expended so much time and charm on her for any reason other than business? He had set her up, taken advantage of her no doubt transparent susceptibility, confident that he could easily persuade her to start work earlier than the date they had agreed upon.

"Cousin Richard is certainly on the ball," she said sweetly. "Lucky for you that Michi will be able to show them around."

"Michi is too busy, Lani. You'll have to do it."

Lani glared at him defiantly. "Oh, no! We had an agreement, Daniel Reid. I'll start work when Brian starts camp, and not one day sooner."

"You'll start work a week from Tuesday. The Mayakawas arrive from Maui next Monday afternoon. The following week you're entertaining an Australian businessman with a wallet the size of the outback. It isn't open to argument."

"You're darn right it isn't!" Lani exploded. "We made a deal. You can't . . ."

"That was before I knew we had a pair of heavy-weights on the agenda," Daniel cut in firmly. "Be reasonable, Lani."

"And what am I supposed to do with Brian? Throw

him out, like yesterday's newspaper? Maybe you don't care about him, but I happen to . . ."

"That's enough, Lani!" Lani's whole body jerked in alarm as Daniel's fist came smashing down on the table. Never had she seen him so close to losing control of himself, and when he spoke again, his voice was low with fury. "The issue isn't Brian. Linda starts work a week from Monday, but if there's any problem, Michi's daughter Sarah will look after him. *Brian* will be fine. The issue is you and your response to me. I was hoping that you'd finally gotten past that knee-jerk reaction of yours—that everything I do is wrong, that my motives are always the worst. But obviously you haven't."

"Nobody likes being made a fool of," Lani replied stiffly. "The only reason you took me to lunch was to turn on the Prescott charm because you wanted something from me. Next time, why don't you try asking? It might save a lot of your time."

"We'd better get out of here before I do something both of us will regret," Daniel growled. He pulled Lani up by the wrist and didn't release her until they had reached the garage. "In!" he ordered, holding the passenger door of the Mercedes open for her.

Although smarting from his rough treatment, Lani held her tongue. She was afraid that if she challenged Daniel again he would either shake her senseless or turn her over his knee and wallop her into submissiveness. Neither prospect held much appeal.

Her nervousness increased when he passed by his house and took the cut-off leading up to Diamond Head Crater, parking the car in the visitors' lot inside the gently bowl-shaped extinct volcano. A smattering of tourists were hiking across its grassy slopes toward the distant rim.

"Would you like to take a walk?" Lani searched Daniel's face warily, looking for some sign of mockery or anger. Finding none, she nodded her agreement, relieved that his anger had cooled.

After strolling for several minutes he eased himself down onto the grass and smiled up at her. "Care to join me?" he invited affably.

It looked rather incongruous to see Daniel sprawled out on the lawn in his blue business suit, and Lani couldn't help but return his smile. She sat down beside him, carefully spreading the light cotton fabric of her dress to prevent grass stains.

"What's so funny?"

Lani giggled at the irritation in his tone. "You. You're so urban. You look funny, lying on the grass in a suit." She plucked a blade and sniffed at it. "It smells so fresh. It's beautiful up here."

"Ah, at last something we can agree on. We both like grass. It smells good, and it's great for golf courses, tennis courts, and parks, not to mention picnics. Also for making love on," he added wickedly.

"Which you would know all about," Lani inserted rather sourly, because she suspected Daniel was amusing himself at her expense.

"Which I would know all about," he agreed blandly. "It's also not a bad place for explanations and apologies."

"Oh?" It was all Lani could manage. Was the arrogant Daniel Prescott Reid actually going to apologize to her for the second time in one day?

"I didn't set you up. I took you to lunch because I wanted to tell you about the hotel. You seemed to be in one of your rare receptive moods so I brought up the

Mayakawas' visit. There was nothing sinister or manipulative about it."

"Did you have to make it an order? Couldn't you just have asked me?" Lani asked plaintively.

"I intended to. I was trying to explain the situation first, but you jumped on me so fast I never had a chance to ask you anything. I figured you'd refuse, so I decided not to give you that option."

Lani had picked several more blades of grass and began absent-mindedly to split them lengthwise. She was thinking about several of Daniel's remarks: "I'm so used to the way you've always gibed at me," and "I was hoping you'd finally gotten past that knee-jerk reaction of yours." Was her image of him—aloof, impervious, and manipulative—terribly shallow and unfair? But before she could say anything, the tickling sensation of grass against her arm startled her into looking up. Daniel was studying her with intent gray eyes. He stopped teasing her arm as soon as he had her attention.

"I could use your help, princess. Please. What about the Mayakawas?"

Lani didn't really want to refuse, but some streak of mischievousness prompted her to ask, "And if I say no?"

"Daring me to force you?" he drawled.

"You couldn't!"

"Okay, so I couldn't," was the temperate reply. But Lani suspected that he probably could.

"And the Australian with the huge wallet? Where does he come into it?"

"I threw him in for the sake of negotiations," Daniel admitted with a laugh. "I'll take one for two, if it's all I can get, princess."

The situation was becoming too intimate for Lani to

handle. The soft breeze, Daniel sprawled out only inches away from her, the sensuous sound of his voice . . . it was increasingly difficult to keep her mind on the conversation. Lani found her thoughts drifting back to his greeting at the airport, and the way his mouth had felt when it brushed her lips. And earlier today, when he had pulled her back against him, he had aroused emotions she had had to struggle to conceal. Daniel was so experienced that touching a woman's body that way probably had little effect on him, and he was so naturally and unconsciously sensual that he could have no idea of the havoc he wreaked every time he so much as spoke to her. He knew she was attracted to him, of course, but would probably have been shocked by the intensity of her physical response.

All the same, she told herself thoughtfully, he had never taken advantage of her—not since that evening seven years ago, and then only to teach her a lesson. Perhaps she had been absurd to be so frightened of him all these years. It was true that she didn't trust herself to be sensible about him, but then, she probably didn't have to. She could trust *him* instead. In any event, the defense system which had worked so well in California didn't seem to work at all in Hawaii, and she much preferred this new teasing, friendly relationship to the old wary hostility.

She stood up and smoothed her dress, shyly extending her hand when Daniel held his out for help in getting up, not that he really needed it. "I'll have to talk to Brian first," she said. "But I'm sure he won't mind."

A single dark brow arched in inquiry. "Japan *and* Australia?"

"Sure."

Only then did his lips curve slowly upward into a devastating, triumphant smile that made Lani tingle and bristle at the same time. Daniel put his arm around her shoulder as they walked to the car, obviously well-pleased with the afternoon's labors.

Chapter Six

On Saturday morning, Daniel took Lani and Brian out to buy a car. He was exceptionally accommodating, merely reminding Lani that the car she selected must seat five adults comfortably, then leaving the choice up to her. Ultimately they agreed on a large Mercedes which handled easily while providing a smooth ride.

"And the color, Mr. Reid?" The showroom manager had dismissed the salesman who had first approached them; Daniel seemed oblivious to his fawning manner, but then he was probably so accustomed to such treatment that he no longer noticed it.

Lani motioned toward a blue model with fawn-colored upholstery. "That's a nice combination," she said.

The manager looked uncomfortable. "I'm terribly sorry, Miss Douglas, but we only have this one in stock.

And it's for another customer. He's coming in Monday to pick it up. I promise I'll have another one for you in less than two weeks."

"We'll need the car immediately," Daniel said firmly. "I want Miss Douglas to spend the next week driving it, getting completely accustomed to it."

"Perhaps you would take a demonstrator in the meantime?" the manager quickly offered. "They're all . . ."

"I really don't care what color it is, Daniel," Lani cut in. She thought the entire discussion was silly. "I'll take whatever they have in stock."

He ignored her comment completely, asking the manager, "The blue car, who's it for?"

By now the man was perspiring lightly, his face twisted into a seemingly permanent worried frown. Even Lani recognized the name he murmured; Robert Bradley was another powerful Hawaiian businessman, like Daniel, a descendant of royalty and missionaries.

Her stepbrother's nod was aristocratic. "I'll see what I can arrange. May I use your phone?" He didn't bother to wait for a reply, but simply strode into the man's office and took possession of his desk.

Such lordly assertiveness was wholly outside Lani's experience, and she listened in bemusement as Daniel placed the call, cheerfully explaining the situation to the man on the other end of the line. "No," he was laughing, "I won't close the Maunalua Bay if you agree. But I'll have my stepsister give you a personal guided tour." There was a brief pause. "5'4", about a hundred pounds, dark auburn hair, blue eyes. She's spectacular, Rob." Daniel listened for several more moments, still smiling, then said, "Okay, Rob, you've got yourself a deal. Why don't you confirm it with Atkins?"

He handed the phone to the manager, who emitted a stream of "Yes sirs," and "Thank you, sirs" and looked very relieved indeed when he hung up the phone.

A short time later Lani was seated behind the wheel of her new car, following Daniel out of the parking lot. As she drove, she wondered just what kind of "deal" Robert Bradley had offered, and why her beauty or lack of it had come under discussion. Did Daniel really think she was "spectacular"? The thought was as potent as a caress.

Unable to contain her curiosity, she pulled her car alongside Daniel's Mercedes in the garage, and blurted out through the open window, "What deal?"

She was certain that his quizzical look was an affectation. "What deal?" he repeated, his eyebrows knitted together in apparent puzzlement.

"With Robert Bradley. About the car!" Lani prompted.

There was a lazy shrug before he opened the door and stepped out of the car, Brian behind him. "Oh, *that* deal. It's nothing much. He wants to spend the night with you in return for letting you have the car."

"Daniel!" Of course he was teasing, and it was ridiculous of her to play into his hands by blushing like a schoolgirl.

"He's taking you out to dinner two weeks from tonight, princess. Is that okay?" Even though Daniel had burst out laughing after her initial shocked reaction, Lani managed to forgive him.

"As long as it's not dinner for two in his bedroom," she replied.

Brian had begun to giggle, though Lani was quite sure that the conversation was miles above his head. Now Daniel chased him into the house, taking Lani's arm and saying in a dry tone, "The only way I'd let you alone with Rob in his bedroom is if he were either unconscious or tied up!"

Lani saw almost nothing of Daniel after they finished lunch. He had secluded himself in his second-floor office, while she had taken Brian out to the tennis court and vollied the ball back and forth with him. Afterward they went for a walk on the beach, and Lani explained to her little brother that Daniel thought she should begin working the following week.

"He does?" Brian was silent for several moments, then said, "Then you have to, if Daniel says so."

"Do you mind, honey?"

"Is Linda gonna take care of me?"

Lani nodded. "Is that all right with you?"

"She's nice." There was another pause. "Besides, if Daniel says so, then you'd better." As far as he was concerned, the matter was decided: Daniel was the boss, and his wishes were to be obeyed.

If ever there was a strong male role model, Lani thought with amusement, it was Daniel Reid. It was probably just as well, little boys had a way of becoming difficult to handle as they grew up, and Daniel would keep Brian under firm control.

It was late afternoon by the time they returned to the house; Daniel appeared in the kitchen just as they were sitting down to drink some lemonade. He was dressed in a dark dinner jacket, ruffled white shirt, and black tie, and looked so strikingly handsome that Lani had to keep her eyes on her drink or risk staring at him in amazement.

"I've been drafted by an old friend as a substitute escort this evening," he told Lani. "It's a charity dinner-dance chaired by Elizabeth's mother, so she has to put in an appearance. Her date is stuck in Hong Kong on business. I really didn't plan to use my ticket, princess. I'm sorry."

Lani seized upon a single word of the explanation. "Elizabeth?" she questioned.

"Elizabeth Thomas. As in Prescott & Thomas. You'll meet her in two weeks. I mentioned a wedding the other day, remember? Her brother, Everett, is the one who's getting married." He held out a ten-dollar bill. "Take Brian out for burgers."

"Inflation isn't *that* bad, yet," she joked, taking the bill from him. "Will you be late?"

He shrugged. "There's a private party afterward. I suppose I'll have to go along to placate Elizabeth. Don't wait up for me." He lifted Brian up and stood him on the dinette chair to give him a hug. "Take care of your sister, superstar," he instructed.

They spent a quiet evening in the library, Lani sorting through travel brochures and guide books while Brian watched his favorite shows on television. The child cajoled her into piggybacking him up the stairs, and as Lani carried him she told herself that he was becoming much too heavy for her to tote around this way. He wasn't a baby anymore, she thought sadly.

Afterward she returned to the library with a cup of hot chocolate and outlined her plans for the following week. She would have to familiarize herself with the layout of the city streets and revisit the popular tourist attractions she had last seen as a child.

It was one o'clock when she finally went up to bed, but there was no sign of Daniel. Only a few nights before he had remarked that people were accustomed to seeing him with beautiful women, "like Michi and Elizabeth." She wondered if the aristocratic Elizabeth Thomas was as stunning as Michi Hansen. Tommy

Prescott had told her that his mother was a Thomas. Were marriages between the two families a common occurrence, and if so, was Daniel considering following in his cousin Richard's footsteps? For some reason, Lani found it a highly disagreeable idea.

She tried to sleep, but succeeded in snatching only a series of fitful catnaps. She kept dreaming of Daniel embracing Elizabeth—whom she pictured as a red-lipped, black-haired temptress—and invariably jerked awake again.

As the hours passed and there was no sound of a car in the driveway, Lani became increasingly disturbed. It was so late—suppose something terrible had happened to him? Like any resort area, Oahu had its share of tough characters who would find Daniel's oversized Mercedes a tempting target for mayhem. By three o'clock she resigned herself to worried sleeplessness, switched on her bedside lamp, and started to read a paperback history of Hawaii.

After an interminable half-hour, the glare of head-lights made moving shadows on the walls of her dimly lit room. Lani threw back her covers and trotted to the staircase, oblivious to how much of her body was revealed by the baby doll pajamas she wore. After a minute the downstairs hall light was clicked on and Daniel came into view. He was clad only in navy blue trunks with a gold stripe down each side; around his neck was slung a damp towel, and over his arm he carried his shirt, suit and shoes.

"I was worried about you!" Lani cried as he climbed the steps. "Do you know what time it is?"

"I told you I'd be late." For some reason, Daniel seemed to be irritated by her presence. "Go to sleep, Lani."

Lani refused to be intimidated by his domineering

tone. She stood her ground until he reached the top, then told him, "All right, *Mr.* Reid. Then when I go out with Robert Bradley, I'll stay out as long as I want, and I won't call you no matter how late I'm going to be!"

There was an exaggerated sigh. "Were you waiting up to join me? Because if you were, I don't care for your taste in nightclothes. You look like a little girl."

"Unlike Elizabeth!" Lani felt like biting her tongue. Why on earth had she said that?

She was further embarrassed by how much the comment seemed to amuse him. "Elizabeth doesn't sleep in anything," he said with a lazy smile. "Take my word for it . . . I know."

"I'll bet you do!" Lani turned on her heel and stormed off into her room.

But once she was alone in bed, a forlorn sigh escaped her lips. What was the use of pretending that she was anything but bitterly jealous of Elizabeth Thomas, Michi Hansen, and any other woman Daniel so much as looked at? Seven years had passed since she had last seen him in a bathing suit, but she remembered exactly how he had looked. There had been a certain boyishness to him that summer, a less threatening, more youthful masculinity. He had matured during the interim, and at thirty-two carried an aura of rugged male power that would have frightened her when she was fifteen. Now it both fascinated and aroused her.

How would it feel to have those hands stroke her body, intimately caressing the most secret of places? To lie in bed next to him, without even the thinnest cloth barriers between them, pressed close together? She remembered their kiss only too well, and the way his tongue had probed her mouth, but now she was old enough to know that there were other parts of her body he could kiss as well. Would she enjoy that?

Good heavens, how could she have pretended to herself all these years that she was anything but wildly and passionately in love with him? Her coldness was a defense mechanism, her taunts an unconscious attempt to provoke him into showing something besides aloof tolerance of her. It was obvious that he didn't return her feelings. How could he? She had caused him nothing but trouble since she was fifteen, rejecting his offers of help, spitting out sarcastic digs at his family, criticizing his company, and automatically disagreeing with every viewpoint he expressed. It was a miracle he had put up with as much as he had. Probably it was for Jonathan's sake.

But what about now? Lani wondered. When Daniel teased her and smiled at her, was it because of some promise to his late father? Or did he really have some feelings for her? And even if he did, how could she possibly compete with a no-doubt enticing creature like Elizabeth Thomas, or the intelligent, beautiful Michi Hansen?

After such a restless night, Lani was not surprised to wake up closer to lunchtime than breakfast. She walked across the hall to Brian's room, found it empty, and glanced out the window overlooking the back of the house. Daniel and Brian were out on the tennis court; her stepbrother, laughing and trotting after the ball, showed no sign of the previous night's revels.

By the time Lani dressed and went downstairs for something to eat, the tennis lesson was over and the two were in the kitchen drinking iced pineapple juice. Daniel suggested brunch at the Maunalua Bay Hotel

and the food turned out to be as scrumptious as it was
bountiful. Afterwards, he dropped Lani and Brian off
at the beach on his way to the office, where he intended
to spend the afternoon working.

Over the next week, Lani found out that Daniel
devoted far more than the usual eight hours per day to
his job. He generally left for the office before she was
even out of bed, usually preparing breakfast for Brian
as well as himself. Although the child was up with the
sun, he went down with it, too. To Lani's disappointment, however, there were no intimate evenings spent
alone with Daniel.

Frequently he was out at business meetings or civic
functions; when he was home he would seclude himself
in his study after dinner to work. Their only contact
was at evening meals, and Brian was inevitably bursting
to relate the day's events, thereby keeping the conversation innocuous and impersonal.

It was a busy week for Lani. She obtained her local
driver's license, stocked up on groceries, and gave the
house a light cleaning. Then she began methodical
preparations for her job as a tour guide. Each morning
she and Brian set out to sightsee, Lani working her way
through a list of attractions she felt she should visit. By
Friday she was able to find her way around the area
with little difficulty, in spite of the city's many one-way
streets and dead ends. Each afternoon she took Brian
to the beach, a reward for his good behavior on these
morning expeditions.

On Friday, Daniel flew to Hilo on the Big Island for a
weekend conference; he did not return until Sunday
night. Lani knew that Michi Hansen would be accompanying him, and wondered if the couple planned to
mix pleasure with business. Jealousy gnawed at her as
she pictured the two of them together.

It might have been a tedious weekend save for Tommy Prescott's undemanding company. He had called on Friday night to invite Lani and Brian to join him for a coastal tour in his parents' cabin cruiser the next day. Lani offered to fix a picnic lunch, and early the next morning Tommy picked them up and drove them out to the marina near Ala Moana Park.

They headed toward Diamond Head, cruising past the tall hotels and apartment houses which rose like concrete stalagmites out of the sands of Waikiki Beach, and rounding the gentle point of land holding the crater that got its name when nineteenth-century sailors mistook calcite crystals for precious diamonds. As the boat purred past the shores of the Kahala District, Lani automatically picked up Tommy's field glasses to look for Daniel's house. Although it was largely hidden by vegetation, the property had a substantial, important air about it—as befitted the millionaire who owned it, Lani thought sourly.

Soon afterwards the Maunalua Bay Hotel came into sight, the building dominating the hillside upon which it rested. The view was an impressive one, with the emerald golf course providing a dramatic backdrop for the fifteen-story stone, steel and glass tower. They travelled around Koko Head Crater, cruised up the northeast side of the island, and then headed back.

The picnic lunch was doubly delicious given the sunlit perfection of the weather and the calmness of the sea. Lani was happy and relaxed in Tommy's company, but couldn't help comparing him to his cousin. Whereas Daniel was mature, self-assured, and carried great responsibilities thoughtfully and gracefully, Tommy was still a basically hedonistic young man who had no greater goal in life than to amuse himself. He was aware that one day he would have to toe the mark, so for the next few years he wanted no commitments at all. Certainly he was amusing, but he was also rather juvenile.

Linda Wong moved in on Monday, aided by her two wiry teenaged brothers. Lani's initial favorable impression was reconfirmed by the easy rapport Linda soon established with Brian. It was lovely to have some free time, and she took full advantage of it, driving over to the Ala Moana shopping center and purchasing half a dozen outfits she felt she would need for her new job, as well as a dress for Everett Thomas's wedding.

Daniel had assured her that she needn't be apprehensive about attending the celebration. Still, a raft of Prescotts and Thomases would be present, as well as many of Hawaii's *kamaainas*—old-line, established citizens. Lani wanted to look her best; even with Daniel by her side she was bound to feel insecure in the company of such people, who probably considered her an insignificant little mainland *haole* in spite of her position as Daniel's stepsister.

Her ultimate choice was a classically simple Grecian-style gown in a cool mint-green that accentuated the flaming highlights in her hair. The ankle-length, full-skirted dress was wrapped at the waist and across the bodice with a gathered swath of material, which ended in a soft bow on one shoulder, leaving the other shoulder alluringly bare.

Michi Hansen called late that afternoon, asking that Lani join her and the Mayakawas for dinner, in order to discuss an itinerary. Lani agreed to meet them at the entrance of the Koolau Room in the hotel.

She put on one of the dresses she had purchased earlier in the day, a street length print with leaves and occasional rose-colored flowers against an off-white background. It had a pleated bodice, square neckline, and cinched belt, all of which made her look as delicate as the frangipani blossoms on her dress.

Armed with guidebooks and brochures, Lani arrived at the hotel elevators just as Michi Hansen and the Mayakawas came walking down the corridor from the direction of the manager's office. By the time everyone was seated in the restaurant, they were chatting companionably in Japanese; Lani was relieved to find that she could keep up with the conversation. Although Mr. Mayakawa was fluent in English, his wife had never progressed beyond an introductory course in high school. Their manner was politely formal as they thanked her in advance for her services as a guide.

Lani suggested a leisurely itinerary, aware that the couple's six year old daughter, presently in their suite with a babysitter, would be joining them when they went sight-seeing. Tuesday was reserved for a drive around the Honolulu area with stops at several popular attractions; Wednesday she planned a trip to the Polynesian Cultural Center on the north shore of Oahu; and Thursday Michi had arranged for a tour of Iolani Palace and a cruise to Pearl Harbor, where a relative of Mr. Mayakawa's had died in the war.

After dinner, Michi led everyone next door to the nightclub to watch the early show. The Mayakawas excused themselves to check on their daughter, and Lani took advantage of their absence to ask Michi, "How can a hotel this size support so many restaurants?"

Her glance swept the large nightclub; patrons filled every table, finishing their buffet meals or sipping exotic tropical drinks. The Koolau Room had been booked to capacity as well, and as she walked into the hotel, Lani had noticed that the Bay Terrace, where she and Daniel had lunched the previous week, had also attracted substantial business.

"The nightclub is a concession," Michi explained. "Mr. Kent rents the facilities from us, but every aspect of the operation is under his control." Lani knew that Jimmy Kent had played everywhere from London to Nashville to Vegas, his easy manner, good voice, and talent as an instrumentalist winning him fans all over the world. "He approached Daniel last year, shortly after he moved to Hawaii permanently. He felt that his personal life was suffering from so much touring."

"So he decided to open his own club," Lani replied. "Judging from the billboard, the show is a combination of country music and Polynesia. Does it work?"

Michi laughed lightly. "Strange bedfellows, I know, but people love it. You'll see." An almost imperceptible nod summoned one of the waiters, Michi ordering a bottle of wine for the table. "As for the chef in the Koolau Room, Daniel enticed him away from a three-star Paris restaurant," she continued. "We attract diners from the Waikiki hotels as well as many local residents, but there's more prestige than profit in the operation. We couldn't possibly accommodate our guests without keeping the Bay Terrace open for dinner."

The show started moments after the Mayakawas returned to the table, and Lani was so delighted by the lavishly staged, rollicking confrontation between Jimmy Kent's downhome country boy and the talented troupe of Polynesian singers and dancers that she failed to notice the approach of a tall, dark-suited figure. When Daniel's hands dropped lightly onto her shoulders she jumped, abruptly twisting around in her seat, her flying elbow nearly knocking over her drink.

"How dare you sneak up on me that way? Or is it too much to ask that you give some warning of your illustrious presence?" Lani spoke angrily but quietly; she didn't want either the Mayakawas or Michi Hansen to see how upset she was. "You ought to be a spy; you have a positive talent for the work."

In reply, he leaned over and whispered in her ear, "I have a lot of talents you haven't discovered, including a few that require an intimate demonstration. Interested, princess?"

Lani shook her head and murmured, "No," but the denial was an outright lie. When Daniel's breath had fanned her neck, his mouth momentarily touching her lobe, it had been impossible to think of anything except the "intimate talents" he had teasingly mentioned. It was quite dark in the nightclub and there was probably no danger of his noticing the pink flush on her face, but Lani turned her head away just the same. Her eye caught Michi's and the older woman smiled at her, apparently in sympathy. There was no hint of jealousy over Daniel's attentiveness, but then Michi was probably very sure of his feelings for her.

After the show everyone remained at the table to talk, and in deference to Mrs. Mayakawa, Lani and Michi continued to use Japanese rather than English. Lani thought with satisfaction that she had finally found something that Daniel *couldn't* do. Linguistic ability was clearly not one of his strong points, and although Michi provided an abbreviated translation there were times when he lost track of the conversation. At other times he and Mr. Mayakawa sat with their heads together, apparently engaged in high-level business negotiations.

Lani had seen a different side of the man she loved tonight, and she was impressed. Many people would have been upset or annoyed to be excluded from a discussion. Lani had never doubted that the godlike Daniel Prescott Reid was in fact human, but had occasionally wondered if anyone had ever bothered to let *him* in on the secret. She found his vulnerable side endearing.

They drove back to the house in separate cars, and as they walked into the kitchen, Lani asked, "Did you nail down Mayakawa's convention?"

He was so obviously puzzled by the question that she went on, "After the show . . . you were talking so earnestly."

"We just met. He knows why we invited him—there'll be time to talk business after he returns to Tokyo. We were discussing family, tradition, that sort of thing. It's something we have in common." He paused. "What about you? Did you get the itinerary settled?"

Lani outlined their tentative schedule as they climbed the steps, mentioning that she had suggested a leisurely pace because the couple's little daughter would be joining them.

Daniel nodded. "That sounds all right. Just make sure you remember that for the next few days you're a tour guide, not a babysitter. You stay with the Mayaka-was and let Brian stay with Linda, princess."

Lani was deeply hurt by this gratuitous if gentle reminder, but merely nodded and went off to her room. How could Daniel think she would purposely disregard his wishes? They hadn't fought in over a week now—not a single angry stare had been exchanged between them. And perhaps, she thought dejectedly, that state of affairs suited him perfectly. Even if he was fond of her, he had no interest in her love—only in her compliance.

Chapter Seven

Lani woke up unusually early the next morning, full of nervous anticipation about her first day of work, and left for the hotel at 9:20 even though she wasn't scheduled to meet the Mayakawas until 10:00.

She filled the extra twenty minutes by talking to Michi Hansen; they had met in the lobby and the manager had quickly invited Lani into her office for a cup of coffee. They chatted about upcoming VIP visitors, with Michi suggesting that Lani stop by at the end of the day to report on how things had gone.

Lani smiled and said she would look forward to it, then walked over to the Mayakawas' suite. A doll-like little creature with coal black hair and huge brown eyes answered her knock.

"Good morning, Miss Douglas." The child enunciated each syllable carefully. "My name is Noriko."

Lani bent down to the little girl's level. "I'm very happy to meet you, Noriko. Are you ready to go for a ride all around Oahu?" This question was greeted by such a wide-eyed, solemn look that Lani realized that the carefully rehearsed speech of welcome had been memorized for the occasion. She smiled and repeated her comments in Japanese, and this time Noriko's head bobbed up and down.

A few moments later the elder Mayakawas came downstairs. Lani settled everyone into the car, her route following the coastline in a counter-clockwise direction. They stopped at a lookout past Koko Head Crater, admiring a placid vista composed of two small off-shore islands, Rabbit Island and Turtle Island, which lay beyond the narrow channel of ocean. The colors of the sea dazzled the senses with their variety and beauty, ranging from a gemlike turquoise near the coast to a smoky, almost purple-blue farther out. Mr. Mayakawa, camera slung around his neck, snapped several pictures of the view.

They continued to hug the coast until reaching the beachside bedroom community of Kailua, and lunched in a little coffee-shop located in a local shopping center.

Afterward, Lani turned inland toward Nuuanu Pali, a historical site high above the towns of Kailua and Kaneohe, with the Pacific Ocean lying beyond. Nearly two hundred years before, Kamehameha I, the king who had unified the Hawaiian Islands, had driven the forces of a rival ruler over this one-thousand-foot cliff in the Koolau Mountains. Now a monument and a concrete observation platform marked the site of his victory, the dramatic view perhaps the loveliest on the island with the lush valley below and the cloud-shrouded mountain peaks above.

As they drove down from the highlands, the bucolic

isolation of Pali gradually gave way to the suburban sprawl of greater Honolulu. When Mrs. Mayakawa complimented Lani on her "charming Japanese accent," she found herself explaining her family background. They knew that she was Daniel Reid's stepsister, and now Lani added that her real father had been killed in an explosion when she was five years old. He lay buried beside more than twenty thousand other American servicemen and women in the National Memorial Cemetery of the Pacific.

The cemetery was known locally as Punchbowl, because it lay within the gently concave one hundred twelve acre floor of a long-extinct volcano which they would pass on their way back to the hotel. The Mayakawas requested that Lani stop briefly.

As they toured the memorial building with its massive stairways bordered by marble walls listing thousands of Americans missing in action, she felt a sudden urge to visit her father's grave. Of course, she had occasionally accompanied her mother to Punchbowl as a child, but remembered feeling little emotion at the time. James Douglas had been at sea so much of the time that her recollections of him were hazy at best.

She could imagine Daniel's disapproval of such a personal pilgrimage during working hours, and decided to come back later in the week. But it seemed that Mrs. Mayakawa had noticed her wistful expression as she stared out over the acres and acres devoted to lives cut short by war or the threat of it. She whispered something to her husband, who turned to Lani and said in his quiet, almost accentless English, "We would like to spend more time here. Perhaps you would pick us up in half an hour?"

Lani smiled and thanked him. But several minutes later, as she stood looking at her late father's name chiseled into a cold slab of stone, it was Jonathan Reid she thought of. It was impossible to grieve over James Douglas, he was only as real to her as the framed wedding portrait she kept on her dresser, next to a similar picture of her mother and Jonathan. It was Jonathan whom she missed, all the more because she had no flesh-and-blood reminder of him. Brian resembled her slim, blonde-haired mother and was a living validation of Anne's existence. As for Daniel, she could see nothing of Jonathan in him, only the patrician looks of the beautiful, spirited Laura and her curmudgeonly father, Thomas Prescott, Senior.

She rejoined the Mayakawas, her thoughts still far away, and drove them up to an observation point near the crater's rim for a view of Honolulu and the harbor. Mrs. Mayakawa then asked Lani to stop at a store featuring colorful Polynesian "aloha fashions" to buy as presents for her nieces and nephews in Japan.

The dual-level Ala Moana shopping center was on their way home, and would provide many stores from which to choose. The Mayakawas decided to shop on their own, giving Lani nearly two hours to herself.

She strolled down the mall, thinking about the Maunalua Bay's Fourth of July Luau. It was less than two weeks away, and she really had nothing suitably Polynesian to wear. A window display of swimsuits and matching cover-ups caught her eye and she went into the shop to investigate further. After trying on several outfits she chose a strapless suit and matching sarong skirt in a brilliant shade of red, appropriately printed with bronze-leafed, pink-flowered ti leaf plants. As long as she was standing still, the side-tied wrap skirt was quite demure, but when she moved a seductive length of leg was revealed. Although concerned about Daniel's reaction, she told herself that she was in

Hawaii now, and most of the women would no doubt be dressed far more daringly.

After dropping the Mayakawas back at the hotel and making a brief stop in Michi's office, Lani returned home to be welcomed by the succulent aroma of braised beef ribs. The table was already set, and Brian was in the library watching television. Linda Wong handed Lani a glass of iced lemonade as soon as she walked in the kitchen, and she felt as pampered as her royal namesake must have been.

Daniel walked in the door just as they were sitting down to dinner. Linda bolted up from the table with an offer to fetch him a drink, which he accepted with such a charming smile that a hard-bitten spinster would have been smitten. Linda was utterly beguiled. For a few minutes he and Lani discussed her day with the Mayakawas, and then he turned his attention to Linda, acting as though nothing could possibly be more fascinating to him than to discover every single fact about his new housekeeper. Lani supposed he was merely attempting to judge her suitability, but few females would be able to resist the seductive style of cross-examination he employed. She wondered jealously just how many women sat by the phone and waited for him to call.

On Wednesday, after having a cup of coffee with Michi, Lani collected the Mayakawas for the hour-long drive to the Polynesian Cultural Center at Laie, on the north shore of Oahu.

The Center, a non-profit living museum, housed reconstructions of seven south sea island villages depicting the traditional lifestyles of the natives of Samoa, New Zealand, Fiji, Tahiti, Hawaii, the Marquesas, and Tonga.

After a canoe tour through the entire area, they walked to the Samoan village. Although there was something deeply appealing about going back to nature to live in simple thatched-roof dwellings with mat-covered floors and tapa bark wall-hangings, Lani knew she preferred the comfort of her plush bedroom in Daniel's air-conditioned house.

After touring several of the other villages, they went to an open-air theater to watch a show depicting the musical history of Polynesia. The biggest crowd pleaser was a vigorous Tahitian otea, danced with hips gyrating wildly. Next, they went into the Center' restaurant for a buffet lunch, then took a tram for tours of the remaining villages before leaving for the hotel.

The traffic was sometimes heavy as they drove home, and by the time Lani dropped her guests off, checked in with Michi, and returned to Daniel's, she wanted nothing more than to put her feet up, close her eyes, and rest. She spent several minutes with Brian before Linda chased her upstairs to her bedroom, and just before she fell asleep she admitted to herself that she was becoming thoroughly spoiled by the efficiency of the full-time housekeeper.

Brian shook her awake an hour later with the news that dinner was ready, and that Daniel had just phoned to say he would be eating with Michi Hansen. Although Linda didn't seem to mind the fact that part of her delicious meal would end up as foil-wrapped leftovers, Lani did. She wanted Daniel home with her, not strolling along on a romantically moonlit beach with a sophisticated rival like Michi Hansen.

Lani had no particular desire to see Michi the next morning—she was tired and pale from a restless night and in no mood for coffee-break chats with Daniel's lady love. But morning and afternoon meetings with

Michi had become part of her routine, and she knew her absence would be noted.

The manager answered her knock, took one look at her drawn face, and observed, "You look like I feel. How about some strong black coffee?"

Lani accepted a cup as Michi sighed, "I thought the meeting would *never* end. Usually Daniel gets through these things faster than anyone I know, but last night he seemed distracted, his mind just wasn't on business." She gazed throughtfully at Lani, obviously expecting some enlightenment as to the reasons for Daniel's behavior.

"Well . . . you know . . ." she stammered, "you went to dinner first, and . . . uh . . . maybe his mind was on . . . other things."

"What do you think we were doing at dinner?" Michi's voice was light with laughter. "A problem came up that Daniel wanted to discuss before the meeting. It was hardly one of our more romantic meals!"

The whole subject made Lani acutely uncomfortable, she didn't want to hear about Daniel's relationship with Michi. Perhaps this particular dinner engagement had been strictly business, but what about all their other evenings together?

She finished her coffee and excused herself to pick up the Mayakawas, who had ten o'clock reservations for a tour of Iolani Palace. This beautifully restored building had once served as the official residence of Hawaiian royalty, and the demand for tours was too heavy for Lani to join the group. She had planned to take Noriko to a nearby playground while her parents were inside the Palace, but as they drove into Honolulu she began to suspect that Mr. Mayakawa preferred a different arrangement.

Noriko was becoming rather restless after so many

days of sightseeing, he said in his polite, low-key manner. Perhaps she missed the company of children her own age.

The child was so quiet and well-behaved that Lani was puzzled by his comments. Remembering Daniel's caveat that she was to be a tour guide and not a babysitter, she offered to drop Noriko off at Daniel's house, explaining that their housekeeper would be happy to take care of both Brian and their daughter.

But Mrs. Mayakawa gave a little shake of her head. Surely the girl did not speak Japanese, she said. Lani was about to offer the services of Michi Hansen's daughter when she realized that the couple preferred to be on their own for the day. Her suggestion that she pick up Brian and take both children to the hotel to play was greeted by two wide smiles.

There was a good deal to see in the area around the Palace, including the Hawaiian State Capitol, Honolulu's Chinatown, and the Falls of Clyde, a nineteenth-century ship. The Kewalo Basin, starting point for the Pearl Harbor Cruise, was only a short busride away. At Iolani Palace, Lani took out her map of Honolulu and circled the locations of various attractions, arranging to meet the Mayakawas at the end of their cruise.

Back at the house, she introduced Noriko to Brian and changed into a cotton bikini printed with a tapa cloth motif, and over it, a short-sleeved, ankle-length cover-up before taking the children to the hotel. The language difference proved to be no inconvenience to the two six-year-olds, who communicated via a series of giggles and gestures as they frolicked together in the shallow end of the pool and built castles on the beach.

After the end of a long day, the Mayakawas and their daughter now reunited, Lani was gathering up some toys she had brought along when Michi Hansen sat down at the foot of her lounge chair. "I've been on the phone with Daniel. I happened to mention that I saw you here with the children today, and he seemed rather . . . put out about it. He wants to see you at his office after you take Brian home."

"In downtown Honolulu?" Lani asked. "It will be six o'clock by the time I get there. Anyway, it's probably something to do with my taking care of the kids today, but it's what the Mayakawas wanted."

"Then I suggest you go down and explain that to Daniel," Michi said. "And try not to antagonize him. He's so used to having you disregard his wishes that perhaps it's understandable that he should think the worst."

The manager smiled sympathetically and left the pool area. Lani decided to follow her advice. She wanted Daniel to know that he could trust her, so she dropped Brian off at the house and drove into Honolulu, intent on explaining what had happened.

The twelve-story office building housing Prescott & Thomas, Inc. was almost deserted when Lani walked in, a uniformed guard the only person in the lobby. "Would you be Miss Douglas?" he asked. Lani nodded, and was directed to the eleventh floor. "Mr. Reid's office is to your right. You can't miss it."

A wall of glass greeted her as she stepped from the elevator; the words "Recreation Division" were spelled out in gold lettering to the left of a set of double doors. No beautiful young woman graced the sleek reception desk, and the hum of the central air conditioning was the only noise to be heard. Lani searched for a suitably important-looking door, locating a carved wooden pair at the end of a short corridor. The office carried no identifying sign, but the right-hand door was slightly ajar.

Her sandals made no sound as she walked over the thick carpet that lined the hallway. She peeked inside; Daniel was sitting with his feet propped up on a Victorian mahogany desk, sprawled back into a leather chair. His eyes were closed as he murmured into the mouthpiece of a beige telephone, the modern instrument looking totally incongruous in the antique-furnished office.

Lani slipped inside and took several steps forward, catching the words, "Sorry, sweetheart. I'm out of circulation." Daniel's face wore a lazy smile. Then, the conversation concluded, he opened his eyes, reached out to hang up the phone—and spotted Lani, directly in front of his desk.

His gray eyes iced over as he swung his feet to the floor and stood up, pointing to a spot about three feet away. "Come . . . over . . . here," he ordered, the words punctuated by brief, intimidating pauses.

Let him get the tirade out of his system, Lani told herself tensely. Daniel was obviously in no mood to listen to explanations, no matter how reasonable. She approached the designated patch of carpet with resignation, dismayed to find that her hands were trembling although she had done absolutely nothing wrong.

"Who do you work for?" he demanded, the measured tone only underscoring his anger.

Lani contained the urge to throw herself at Daniel's feet, cringing with repentence as she answered with a sob, "I work for you, O most revered Lord of the Island." Instead she limited herself to a stoic, "The Maunalua Bay Hotel."

"Which is owned by?"

"Prescott & Thomas." Hurt mingled with annoyance. Why was he acting this way? He had no right to make her stand at attention while he cross-examined her like an errant schoolgirl. She wasn't eighteen anymore!

"And which division administers our hotel business?" he continued in a cold voice.

"The Recreation Division," Lani snapped, well and truly aroused now. And Daniel accused *her* of jumping to conclusions!

"And who directs that division?"

"You do!" she exploded, "and if you would listen to me . . ."

"Which makes me your boss," he interrupted harshly, "and when I tell you to do something—or not to do it—you'll damn well obey me. We don't pay you to lounge around the swimming pool with a pair of six year olds!"

It was the perfect opening for Lani to ask, "Not even if the customer requests it?" But she was much too upset, able only to scream, "Then keep your lousy paycheck!" before turning on her heel and storming out of his office.

"You're not going anywhere!" The angry words assaulted her ears at the same moment that Daniel seized her from behind, his hands clamping themselves around her upper arms with very little gentleness.

Lani's instinctive struggles were short-lived. After a moment her head drooped down, her eyes brimming with tears. "Please, Daniel," she said hoarsely, "you're hurting me."

"Auwe!" The Hawaiian exclamation meant Ouch! or Alas! but Lani had no time to consider Daniel's apparent change of mood. He had taken a step forward, so that his body was pressed against her back. He snaked his left arm around her body, until it came to rest on her right shoulder, his forearm pressing lightly against her throat.

While his lips nibbled down the side of her neck, his right hand tugged at the zip front of her cover-up, pulling it down to her navel to allow him access to the softness underneath.

Lani was so shocked that movement and speech seemed impossible. In the past, Daniel had acted seductively or made provocative comments, but he had never actually touched her, not like this. She felt her breasts swell and harden, the nipples like little pebbles even before he slid his hand inside her bikini top.

"Relax, princess." His breath warmed her ear as his teeth teased the lobe. His left arm dropped from her shoulder to her hip, pulling her intimately against his body, and she could feel his insistent masculinity as he molded her against his hard, lean length.

Lani was aware of her heart pounding out of control, of her uneven, labored breathing, of the tingling weakness that made her want to melt against Daniel's body. But how could she? She was terribly in love with Daniel, but he had no such feelings for her. She hadn't meant to provoke him—somehow both of them had simply exploded—and now he was kissing her in anger, just like he had seven years ago. Only this time, she feared, the lesson would end on his office couch.

Torn by conflicting feelings, Lani allowed herself to be touched and caressed, her only response a frightened quivering. Then Daniel slipped his hand down to her stomach, gently stroking the bare skin, and so alarming her that her trancelike state dissolved into whispered pleading. "Please, Daniel. Don't . . ." She was horrified when several tears escaped her eyes.

He slowly released her, backing away to permit her to pull up the zipper of her cover-up and regain her composure. She started violently when, only moments later, he again placed his hands on her arms, turning her around to face him.

"You aren't leaving yet," he stated with grim determination. "Not until I get some response from you."

He lowered his head again, his mouth touching her unresisting lips, stroking them seductively, then lifting, only to descend and repeat the operation a second time . . . a third . . . a fourth. Both his arms stole around her body to hold her with a possessive firmness that brooked no attempts at escape. And by now, Lani was no longer capable of escape. The coaxing, teasing insistence of his mouth, rubbing against her lips, lightly playing with them until she was aching for more, had destroyed her defenses. Her body was feverish with desire, burning every bit of resistance and common sense from her mind. Daniel opened his mouth above hers and gently urged her lips apart, his tongue carefully probing, testing its welcome.

Somehow Lani's hands crept up to slip underneath the open jacket of his suit to hold him around the waist. His kiss deepened into a voyage of exploration, his mouth gentle but passionate in its leisurely, thorough investigations. Lani's fingers curled into fists which clutched at his back. She made no protest when he pressed her body against his own, responding to his movements with a wanton instinctiveness. She heard a low moan and realized with shock that it had come from her own throat.

But Daniel wasn't moaning. His breathing was regular, his hands firm and steady on her hips, his mouth deliberate and controlled on her own. Lani knew relatively little about men, but thought in confusion that if Daniel were in love with her, he would surely be more passionate, more hungry. Good heavens, she was making an utter fool of herself, responding so wildly. She slid her hands from his back, intending to push him away.

He allowed the withdrawal, releasing her as soon as he felt her resistance and then holding her away from him and gazing down at her with amusement in his gray eyes. "Much better, princess," he murmured with a smile. Lani shrugged out of his grip, her face reddening with embarrassment at how easily Daniel had overcome her objections. And now he was laughing at her.

Daniel cocked his head toward a silk brocade-covered couch at the far end of his office. "Sit down. I'll get you a glass of wine."

"I don't . . . that is . . . I think . . . it's getting late, Daniel, and Linda has dinner . . ." Lani wanted only to escape. She couldn't stay here alone with Daniel, let him sit down next to her on the small sofa.

He seemed to read her mind. "I'm not going to take advantage of your willingness, princess. I'll sit in the chair and we'll talk this out." When Lani made no move to obey his command, he asked in a dry tone, "Do you walk there under your own steam, or do I carry you?"

"I walk," Lani said. Her heart was finally beating more normally. She had the feeling that Daniel had gotten what he wanted and wouldn't touch her again.

He handed her a glass of red wine and sat down, as promised, in an adjacent chair. It was obvious that he had no intention of discussing his behavior. "Tell me what you were doing with Brian and Noriko today," he said as he made himself comfortable. He sounded every inch the boss demanding an explanation, but his tone lacked his earlier anger and sarcasm.

Still wary, Lani told him in a careful monotone exactly why she had disregarded his instructions.

"Why didn't you tell me that in the first place?" Daniel asked in exasperation. Lani felt her face heat up defensively, and was about to deliver a heartfelt protest about his propensity to declare her guilty without a trial when he held up a hand to check her. "I didn't give you much of a chance, did I?" he admitted ruefully. "I'm sorry, Lani. It's been a lousy day, and when Michi told me you were with the kids, I was in a mood to decide you'd done it on purpose. I sat here, just waiting to nail you to the floor."

"Oh." Lani took a sip of her wine. Daniel's apology encouraged her to ask him just what he had intended to accomplish by kissing her in such an intimate, insistent fashion. She mentally phrased the question, but even thinking about the wildness of her response made her blush, and it was all she could do to repeat that it was late and Linda would be wondering what had happened to them.

"Don't worry about it. I phoned her before you showed up. She'll keep dinner warm."

He hadn't been talking to Linda Wong when Lani walked into the office. She remembered his words— "Sorry, sweetheart. I'm out of circulation." At the time she had been too tense to do any more than register the phrase, but now she reflected on its meaning. Apparently Daniel had been rejecting an invitation, no doubt from some alluring creature. Was he too deeply involved with Michi Hansen to see anyone else? And if so, how could he possibly justify the advances he had made to Lani? How could she continue to live in the same house with a man who could virtually seduce one woman while supposedly committed to another?

"I think I should get my own apartment, Daniel." She glanced at him to judge his reaction. His face was bland. "I mean, I can't keep living with you," she added rather desperately.

"Really? Why not?" Daniel was smiling as he posed these questions, and Lani's temper began to simmer. Maybe *he* thought the situation was funny, but *she* didn't!

"After . . . after what just happened? You can't be serious!"

"Very little happened," he answered smoothly. "And what *did* happen won't happen again, I promise you. I have no designs on your virtue, Lani. You'll be a virgin on your wedding night, believe me." He stood up. "I'm getting hungry. Let's go home."

Lani complied, handing her glass to Daniel and walking out of the office ahead of him. She had been shattered by his lazy words and couldn't let him see her face. Perhaps to him their romantic interlude had been "very little," but to her it had been overwhelming. She remembered her fantasies about how it would feel if Daniel made love to her, and now she had her answer. If he had loved her, it would have been the most sweetly exciting experience in the world. But he didn't, and the pain of it was so excruciating that she wanted nothing other than the solitude of her room, so she could cry her heart out.

Chapter Eight

Lani had her solitude; she pleaded a headache and went upstairs to her room as soon as they got home. Yet somehow Daniel's immediate expression of concern seemed so genuine that once she was alone, her essentially optimistic nature reasserted itself. After all, the situation wasn't hopeless. True, Daniel didn't love her, but he wasn't making marriage proposals to Michi or anyone else either. She preferred to tell herself that the way she could get under his skin was a positive sign.

She was playing tennis with Brian late Friday afternoon when Linda came outside to fetch her into the house for a telephone call. "His name is Robert Bradley. Would that be *the* Robert Bradley?"

It took a moment for Lani to remember why he was calling. "Yes," she said, and explained to the wide-eyed Linda about the circumstances surrounding the purchase of her car.

Lani wasn't particularly eager to keep their dinner date, but she knew she would need some diversion if she wasn't to succumb to brooding and tears. It would be foolish to sit home alone Saturday night, miserably jealous because Daniel was off enjoying himself with Michi Hansen. She tried to make her voice enthusiastic as she said hello.

"I'm looking forward to meeting you." Robert Bradley's voice was deep and pleasant as he made the conventional reply. "Daniel called me a little while ago to inform me that it was going to be a double date. I don't think he trusts me alone with you."

That little piece of information caused Lani to flush with embarrassment. Daniel had always suspected her of being wanton, and her passionate response on Thursday afternoon must have convinced him how right he was. "It's me he doesn't trust," she blurted out, then bit her lip in regret.

The comment was greeted by laughter. "If you mean that he thinks you're a babe-in-the-woods, you're right. He made a point of reminding me that you're only twenty-two years old. So let me reassure you. I have a fifteen-year-old daughter, Lani. The car is a birthday present for her. I also have a seventeen-year-old son. I'm well aware that you're too young for me."

"Then why take me out to dinner?" The question slipped out before Lani could prevent it.

There was another chuckle. "Mostly to annoy my friend Daniel. Rumor has it that he's pretty protective of you. I hear he almost shipped his cousin Tommy to one of the neighbor islands just to keep him away from you."

Lani smiled for the first time since the previous afternoon. Perhaps a double date wouldn't be so unbearable after all, given the fact that Robert Bradley seemed intent on needling her stepbrother. Daniel couldn't quash an equal as easily as he could Tommy or herself. And he really was an unforgivable hypocrite to insist that other men keep their distance from her when he had done the exact opposite himself—even if his reason had nothing to do with unslakable passion for her.

"Tommy's always been a perfect gentleman," she replied lightly. "Are we meeting you somewhere tomorrow?"

"Michi and I are driving over to your house for cocktails. We're taking Daniel's car to the restaurant. See you tomorrow night, Lani."

"Yes. And thank you for calling." Her farewell was somewhat distant. How could she have overlooked the fact that Daniel would be with Michi tomorrow? She would have to sit at the same table with him for hours, watching him shower another woman with love and attention. Suddenly, she dreaded the entire evening.

It might have been easier if she felt even the slightest disdain or dislike for Michi, but she didn't. Michi was unfailingly warm and friendly to her, increasingly so as they got to know each other better. Obviously she was determined to have a good relationship with her future sister-in-law, Lani thought dejectedly.

As she dressed for her date with Rob the next evening, Lani found herself wishing that it was Sunday afternoon, that she was donning her beautiful new gown in preparation for the wedding of Everett Thomas III. If only the evening were over with! For the past two days she had managed to pretend that Daniel's passionate embrace of the previous Thursday had never happened. She had seen him only at meals, where he directed most of his attention toward Brian. When he deigned to notice Lani he treated her exactly like a kid sister, and she affected a cool nonchalance in return. But she doubted her ability to keep up the facade for an entire evening.

She did not come downstairs until she heard the doorbell ring. When she walked into the living room, Robert Bradley was standing side-by-side with Michi Hansen. His gray-streaked hair and patrician features reminded Lani of an older version of Daniel; Michi, glamorous as always in an apricot-colored silk suit and coordinated blouse, smiled at Lani and complimented her on her outfit. Lani knew she looked attractive in the lemon yellow front-slitted skirt and lemon and white blouse she wore, but the knowledge did nothing to brighten her mood.

Daniel introduced her to Robert Bradley, who immediately draped an arm over her shoulder and led her to the bar. He poured her some sherry, obviously completely at home in his friend's house. Then Linda brought in some Chinese-style hors d'oeuvres and everyone talked shop—the tourist trade—for the next half-hour.

The restaurant was located in one of Robert Bradley's hotels. The two men commandeered the front seat of the Mercedes to talk over a business deal, consigning Lani and Michi to the back. As the evening proceeded, Rob became increasingly attentive, leaning over to talk to Lani in a sensuously soft voice, covering her hand with his own, directing numerous charming smiles her way. If Daniel objected, he gave no indication of it. He seemed far too interested in Michi to notice, and Lani, trying to hide her jealousy, responded to Rob's playacting with far more enthusiasm than she otherwise would have.

She had little appetite for the food, which was

excellent, although not, Daniel insisted, on a par with the Maunalua Bay's Koolau Room. "You're right," Rob agreed with a lazy smile. "My chef's not on a *par* with yours . . . he's better."

The conversation often devolved into such friendly games of one-upmanship, but the competitiveness of the two men didn't prevent them from being business partners as well as close friends. The two companies were holding preliminary discussions concerning a joint development venture on Kauai.

Daniel invited Michi and Rob back to the house for a nightcap, and now Lani found herself seated next to her date on the couch, trying to respond naturally to his loverlike manner. Michi and Daniel were standing next to the piano, apparently lost in a world of their own.

After several minutes Rob took Lani's hand and said in a conversational tone of voice, "When am I going to see you again?"

"You'll see her tomorrow, at the wedding." The curt statement sliced across the room.

"With three hundred other people? I had something more intimate in mind, Daniel," Robert drawled.

"Forget it, Rob. You're old enough to be her father." Daniel took Michi's arm and walked toward the couch. "I'm going to throw you two out; I have an early golf game tomorrow."

Lani maintained a circumspect silence. Robert Bradley was more than capable of holding his own against Daniel; in fact, she suspected that he could be every bit as arrogant as her stepbrother.

He simply ignored Daniel's injunction. "I have to go to the mainland on business for a week, so how about two weeks from tomorrow? Dinner again?"

Lani glanced at Daniel, noticed the look of extreme disapproval on his face, and favored Rob with a glowing smile. "Thank you, Rob. I'd love to," she said. She allowed herself to be helped from the couch and stood submissively while Rob, his back to Daniel, planted a lingering kiss on her mouth. In reality, the embrace was no more than brotherly, but it must have appeared quite passionate from Daniel's vantage point. Lani enjoyed Rob's company, but had no physical reaction when he touched her. Only Daniel was capable of arousing her to the point where pride alone stopped her from giving him whatever he chose to ask of her.

"Whenever you're finished, Rob . . ." Rob lifted his head in response to the impatient words, winking at Lani. "I want a few words with you," Daniel snapped out, taking Rob's arm and leading him into the kitchen.

Lani caught Michi Hansen schooling her features to suppress a smile, and murmured with embarrassment, "He takes the big brother role pretty seriously, he always has."

"But he's not your brother," Michi said, an enchantingly teasing smile on her mouth.

"Try telling *him* that!"

"I don't have to. He's well aware of it," Michi laughed. Lani wondered in confusion just why the other woman was so amused by Daniel's overprotectiveness.

The men returned several minutes later, Daniel looking annoyed, Robert smiling smugly. As soon as polite good-nights had been exchanged and the door shut behind their guests, Daniel looked at Lani with the same steely glare she had last seen on Thursday. "He's not interested in you, you know."

She *did* know, and was not about to claim otherwise. If she challenged Daniel he might retaliate in the same manner as two days ago, and Lani doubted she would stop him, not when she was so in love with him that she spent her nights imagining herself in his arms. She said nothing.

"He knows I don't like it . . . he's doing it to annoy me," Daniel muttered under his breath. Then he added in a louder tone, "Since Rob's wife died three years ago, he's never taken out anyone younger than thirty. As a matter of fact, I thought he was attracted to Michi."

"Would you mind if he asked her out?" Lani could have kicked herself for asking the question. She had sounded far too interested in his answer.

He shrugged. "Why should I mind?"

His reply could only reflect total confidence in the closeness of his relationship with Michi, Lani thought miserably. Given the futility of loving Daniel, it would do her good to go out with Rob, who was entertaining and kind, and who would make no demands on her beyond those of a friend.

"So what did you and Rob decide?" she asked nervously. "Are we going out in two weeks?"

Daniel nodded. "Sure. As long as he understands the situation. But don't expect any hot love scenes, princess. With Rob, business comes before pleasure."

Lani stared up at him in bewilderment. "What are you talking about?"

"Ask Rob. You'll see him tomorrow." With a final, chilly look, Daniel turned around and walked toward the stairs.

On Sunday morning, Linda invited Lani and Brian to attend church with her and her family, and afterward, her tiny, soft-spoken mother asked them back to the house for lunch. Since Daniel would be playing golf until the early afternoon, Lani accepted.

Brian soon disappeared along with Linda's two youngest siblings, and the three children were having such a good time together that Lani stayed far longer than she intended to. It was difficult for her to keep her mind on the conversation with Linda and her parents, because as the minutes dragged by, she became increasingly apprehensive about the wedding she was to attend. Her beloved stepfather had suffered rough treatment at the hands of certain *kamaainas*, and although that was long ago Lani could easily picture herself as the target of their snubs today. Unlike Jonathan, she doubted her ability to smile and turn the other cheek.

She returned home to find that Daniel had scrawled a message on the bottom of her own note to him: he was sailing with his cousin and would be back in time for the wedding.

About an hour later, Lani stood in front of her full-length mirror, her only garment a short terry robe, and inspected her appearance. Her hair fell in graceful waves down her back; her make-up, although subtle, was heavier than usual, adding several years to her appearance. The even tan she had acquired during her first weeks in Hawaii gave her a healthy, attractive glow, and as she studied her face it seemed impossible that only a month before those same features had been pale and haggard with bereavement. Although she had stubbornly resisted each of Daniel's decisions about the future, she was forced to admit that he had been right every time.

Brian was thriving in Hawaii, with Daniel acting as a much-needed father figure. As for herself, had she remained in San Diego and attempted to care for Brian on her own, daily life would have become an exhausting struggle. Instead, she had an almost sinful amount of freedom and a job she adored. She truly loved her native state, and even the ravages of the developers couldn't change her feelings.

But then, she had come to realize that Prescott & Thomas did not represent the ultimate evil in island society. Tourism was now Hawaii's number one industry, providing close to one hundred thousand jobs, nearly a third of all tax revenues, and billions of dollars for the state's economy. How well she remembered the night Daniel had thrown those figures at her head! She had tossed her hair in annoyed acceptance of his expertise and challenged him to join a local environmental group boasting many *kamaainas* as members. To her astonishment, he had quickly agreed to do so.

Two sharp raps on the door interrupted her musings. "Time to go, princess. Are you ready?"

"Give me five minutes," she called out, suddenly aware that she must have been standing in front of the mirror, lost in thought, for a good fifteen minutes. As she stepped into her mint-green gown and silver sandals, she told herself firmly that she would never look any better than she did at this moment. Daniel's subsequent nod of approval, warm and appreciative, helped to boost her confidence.

Her apprehension soon melted away in the face of the charming reception she received. A lavish cocktail buffet and formal dinner followed the religious ceremony; Daniel stood close by her side throughout the cocktail hour, introducing her to an endless stream of smiling relatives, friends, and business associates. Among the first people she met were Tommy Prescott's sister, Hope, his father, Richard, the Chairman of Prescott & Thomas, and his mother, Marilyn Thomas Prescott, who was also the aunt of the groom. Tommy had once promised Lani that she would love his mother, and indeed, Marilyn was one of those warm, vivacious women whom everyone adores on sight.

Robert Bradley and Michi Hansen were also among the guests, these two familiar faces helping Lani to relax and enjoy herself. But then, with Daniel so attentive and protective, how could she fail to have a wonderful time?

Soon after the bride and groom stepped onto the floor to dance to the first waltz, Lani was claimed as a partner by Robert Bradley. The French champagne had flowed like the waters of Waimea Falls, and Lani had drunk several glasses more than her usual quota. The room had a lovely haziness. Her usual inhibitions fled in the face of her curiosity about Rob's conversation with Daniel the previous night, and she asked with a giggle, "What did Daniel mean last night when he told me that you put business before pleasure?"

"He informed me that if I made a pass at you, I could forget the business deal we've been discussing." He pulled her a little closer, then bent his head to whisper in her ear, "Daniel's very possessive, even for an over-protective big brother. I'd say he's in love with you, *princess*." The last word was lightly accented, a mocking reference to Daniel's pet name for her.

"I wish it were . . ." Lani stopped, but not quickly enough. Why had she accepted that last glass of champagne from her stepbrother?

"When you blush like that you're irresistible. I can't blame him for being captivated," Rob teased.

Lani hastened to correct his mistaken assessment. "You're wrong. We've done nothing but fight for years and years. He just thinks . . . that is, he's afraid that I'm going to get myself into trouble, so he watches out for me."

"If you say so, Lani." Robert Bradley had smoothly

rejected her explanation, but he could have no knowl-
edge of her previously frosty relationship with Daniel.
And even if he did care for her a little, there was always
Michi, whom he loved.

After the dance she excused herself and went into the
ladies' room. The conversation had upset her. Robert
Bradley's misinterpretation of Daniel's feelings had
served to remind her of dreams that would never be
fulfilled, and she needed a few moments alone to regain
her composure.

She sat down at the dressing table and began to brush
her hair, noticing in the mirror that the door had
opened to admit a tall, slim blonde. She was dressed in
a black, halter-topped gown slashed to the waist on
each side and slit up to the thigh to reveal matching
toreador pants underneath. Her long silvery hair hung
straight down her back, the gold slave bracelet on her
arm matching her dangling earrings.

"I'm afraid Daniel was remiss in his introductions,"
she said in a purring, husky voice as she sat down next
to Lani to repair her make-up. "I'm Elizabeth Thomas,
the groom's sister."

Lani managed a weak smile. Elizabeth Thomas had
been one of the bridesmaids, but for the ceremony and
pictures she had worn a demure pastel dress, her hair
pinned into a French twist. She had obviously changed
during the cocktail hour, and her present appearance
invited graphic fantasies about what she and Daniel had
been doing the night he had walked in at 3:30 a.m.

Elizabeth reached into her purse for her cigarettes,
lit one, and took a long drag of it. "It's quite a
convenient arrangement Daniel has, with you tucked
away in his house, awaiting his pleasure, running to his
bed whenever he whistles. You *do* look amazingly
innocent, considering, darling," she drawled.

Lani was so appalled by the accusation that she almost dropped her brush. "That's—Daniel would never do that," she choked out.

"Why not? He's human, isn't he? People *do* talk," Elizabeth said viciously, blowing smoke in Lani's face. "And everyone knows you're his latest mistress. But you won't last long. He'll get tired of playing with children." Before Lani could say another word in her own defense, Elizabeth had strolled languidly out of the lounge.

For several seconds Lani was too stunned to move from her seat in front of the mirror, but simply stared at her own pale reflection, seeing nothing. Had Elizabeth spoken the truth, or merely a malicious fabrication designed to upset her? She could think of no reason why the woman would attack her so viciously; she must have been repeating a common item of gossip.

Lani couldn't go back to the reception to face the knowing stares of hundreds of eyes. Neither could she stay in the lounge while women paraded in and out, silently pinning a scarlet A on her chest. Tears were threatening, and she fled in distress into a stall in the bathroom, where no one could see her.

"Lani?"

The voice was Michi Hansen's, and even though Lani had finally managed to control her emotions, she had no intention of answering the summons. She wanted to be left alone.

"Lani, I know you're in there. I can see the bottom of your gown. Either you come out and tell me what's wrong, or I'm going to get Daniel to *drag* you out of there!"

It was a horrifying prospect, and faced with such an unappetizing choice, Lani slowly emerged from the stall.

"I want to go home," she told Michi in a hoarse voice. "Will you drive me home?" And then, to compound her misery, she burst into tears.

Michi led her to the sofa and offered her a tissue. She murmured soothing phrases until Lani managed to contain her tears, then demanded to know what was wrong. Lani refused to say a single word. Michi immediately threatened to fetch Daniel again, and Lani knew anything would be less embarrassing than facing *him*.

"It . . . it was Elizabeth Thomas," she said with a sniff. "She came in here . . . and she said . . . she said everyone thinks that Daniel and I . . . that we . . ."

"That little cat!" Lani was so astonished by the vehemence in the usually unflappable Michi's voice that for a moment she forgot her own unhappiness and simply stared. Then the older woman sighed in exasperation.

"Elizabeth and Daniel spent a rather . . . passionate summer together seven years ago. Everyone expected an engagement, perhaps as soon as Christmas time. Both he and Elizabeth went back to school in New England that fall, but apparently something had happened in the meantime to cool him off. Elizabeth's been chasing him ever since, and she can be downright vicious to anyone she thinks is a threat."

"But that's . . . it's ridiculous," Lani said. "Daniel and I . . . we don't . . . but if everyone *thinks* we do . . . I can't keep living there."

"Now you're being ridiculous," Michi stated firmly. "There's not a person on this island who believes that Daniel Reid would be capable of something so sordid, and that includes Elizabeth Thomas." She smiled in that irresistible, teasing way of hers. "He's much too honorable to import an innocent little *haole* like you to warm his bed, and I hope you won't let Elizabeth's accusations upset you. If you do, you'll only be giving her what she wants."

It was the one argument Michi could have made to persuade Lani to rejoin the celebration; she was far too stubborn to allow some aristocratic island feline to get the better of her. She lifted her chin a fraction higher and told Michi, "All right. Just give me a few minutes to fix my make-up and I'll be right out."

Nonetheless, as Lani re-entered the room she felt as though every head had swung around to follow her progress. She wanted to turn on her heel and run right out again until she noticed Elizabeth Thomas's spiteful look, which angered her into shooting back an icy stare of her own and marching straight to her seat. She had just reached the table when Daniel stood up, took her by the arm, and led her to the dance floor.

Lani attempted to ignore the speculative glances which greeted this maneuver. "Are you all right, princess?" he asked.

"I just . . . I had a little too much champagne," she lied. "I went to the ladies' room to lie down." She didn't want to discuss Elizabeth's accusations at all, and certainly not with her stepbrother.

She heard his low rumble of laughter, his body shaking against hers as they danced to the slow, throbbing music. "Really? Was it vintage 1952, with a silvery color and a frosty bouquet?"

Lani was too embarrassed to manage an answer. Naturally Daniel would have insisted on a full report from Michi.

"Forget it, honey," he continued. "Elizabeth's never been able to accept the fact that I . . ." He paused a moment, then went on, ". . . that I decided not to marry her. Her parents have spoiled her rotten. She needs some guy to take her in hand, but it isn't going to be me."

His arms tightened, pulling her closer in a manner guaranteed to provoke comment. "Please, Daniel," Lani said, squirming uncomfortably. "You're only going to start more gossip."

To her relief, he loosened his grip to look into her eyes, his expression becoming solemn when he read the distress in them. "I promised you that you'd be a virgin on your wedding night, didn't I, princess?" he asked soothingly. "You're my stepsister and my responsibility, and there's absolutely nothing immoral about your living with me . . . not when Brian needs both of us to take care of him. But people *will* have something to talk about if you start acting defensive about it."

He pulled her gently back into his arms, but not too close, and this time Lani did not withdraw. It was much too pleasant to stay in his embrace.

Chapter Nine

During the next few weeks, Daniel was the model of a thoughtful companion. He joined Lani and Brian for dinner most evenings and took them for weekend outings—sailing, to the beach, on picnics. There were no more arguments or harsh criticisms. After dinner he would often remain downstairs to talk to Lani while Brian watched television, and these hours together were the most precious and bittersweet of all.

Daniel spoke of his ideas for possible projects and his personal vision of Hawaii's future, and even mentioned his desire to marry and raise a family. Lani knew that he was confiding his dreams, and she responded with eager interest and a few confessions of her own. She was careful not to reveal her feelings, but did let Daniel see that she was happy in Hawaii. Of course, he would never know what heaven it was for her to feel so close to the man she loved—and what hell to realize that the future he spoke of would be shared with another woman.

Wade Thorpe, Daniel's "Australian with a wallet the size of the outback," flew into Honolulu on Monday afternoon, accompanied by his wife and two sons. Lani was detailed to pick them up at the airport, and during the rest of the week she was kept busy entertaining the strapping Thorpe clan. She continued to drop by Michi's office each morning and afternoon, and as much as she liked the other woman, it was difficult to hide her jealousy behind a pleasant facade each time Michi would mention that Daniel had lunched with her, or was taking her to dinner that night.

Sometimes she permitted herself a dollop of hope, because although Daniel's feelings for Michi were apparent to everyone when he looked at her, Michi was still mourning the loss of her husband. Lani suspected that her feelings for Daniel were no more than gratitude and deep affection for a dear friend. But some day she would be ready for a new love, and perhaps Daniel was determined to wait for her.

The hotel was staging a lavish luau on the Fourth of July, with a gourmet buffet and entertainment by Jimmy Kent. The price of a single ticket exceeded the cost of dinner for two at many fine island restaurants, but even so, the affair was sold out well in advance.

Lani was pleased at how attractive she looked in the strapless suit and sarong she had purchased a few weeks before. The outfit managed to seem sensuous, yet not at all exhibitionistic, and she eagerly awaited Daniel's assessment of her appearance. He was waiting in the hall along with Brian as she descended the stairs, his body encased in fitted jeans and a printed Hawaiian shirt.

For a moment there was such an icy look in his eyes that Lani wanted to run back to her room to change. Then she told herself that his anger must be over something else entirely, because he was suddenly smiling and telling her that she looked very nice. "You'd better go up and get a shawl," he added. "The wind is picking up."

The bar was already doing a brisk business when they arrived. Dozens of long tables had been set up on the lawn between the beach and the pool, and hundreds of guests milled throughout the area, drinks in hand. A portable stage had been erected on the concrete deck of the pool with Jimmy Kent's back-up band playing Hawaiian music interspersed with American favorites. Appropriately, the decorations were red, white, and blue, with matching lights strung in the trees to add a festive air.

Lani recognized a smattering of Prescotts and Thomases from the wedding, including Elizabeth in a halter dress so scanty that she barely managed to stay decent in it. She immediately sauntered over and took possession of Daniel, and Lani soon found herself in a conversation with Tommy's parents, Richard and Marilyn Prescott. They really were wonderful people, she thought to herself. They treated her with great warmth, as if she were a favorite niece.

Brian had gone down to the beach to look for shells along with several of Tommy's younger cousins. Lani gradually relaxed and forgot about Elizabeth as she chatted with the Prescotts. Eventually Richard's parents joined them, and Charles and Mary Prescott were so amiable and friendly that Lani could scarcely believe that they were the son and daughter-in-law of the couple who had so rudely snubbed her stepfather.

The festivities began with a net fishing demonstration, one young man piloting a torch-lit canoe while a second repeatedly flung a large net into the ocean. Next, the traditional kalua or roast pig was removed from the *imu,* an underground, hot rock oven, by two young men clad only in short cloth skirts. The first was a dark-skinned Polynesian, and Lani began to giggle with recognition when she noticed who the other was. "A last minute replacement," Marilyn whispered. "Tommy got drafted when the boy who usually does this came down with chicken pox!"

The buffet tables had been set up inside the Bay Terrace restaurant, which was closed to other business for the evening. In addition to the salty, smoke-flavored kalua pig, there were such traditional dishes as poi, a light purple-colored paste made of pounded taro root and water; pipi kaula, a spicy Hawaiian beef jerky; lomi-lomi salmon, a salty, steamed fish with green onions and tomato; mahimahi, or dolphin fish, not to be confused with the actual dolphins that entertained at marine shows all over the world; beef teriyaki; fresh tropical fruits; and haupia, a puddinglike dessert made from fermented coconut milk. Also on the menu were American favorites like baked ham, fried chicken and various types of pies.

Marilyn helped Lani organize the children at a separate table at one end of the dining area, and then both women took their place in the buffet line. If Lani was dismayed to find Elizabeth Thomas seated at the other end of her table, she experienced a moment of delighted triumph when Daniel joined them, dispossessing Tommy of the seat next to her own. Tommy cheerfully got up, snatched a vacant chair from an adjacent table, and plunked it down next to the sullen Elizabeth.

If any of Daniel's relatives suspected that his relationship with Lani was anything other than respectable, they gave no sign of it. After a few mai tais, Lani was able to ignore Elizabeth's venomous looks and enjoy the good-natured competitiveness and joking between the Prescott and Thomas clans. When she went back to the buffet for dessert she passed by Brian's table; he and his stepcousins were giggling and shouting at each other, and she felt a stab of guilt about her earlier intention to keep him in San Diego. It would have been very selfish of her to deprive him of this extended family, and if she ever returned to the mainland, she knew she would have to leave him with Daniel.

Jimmy Kent's show was dazzling, even if the dancers' costumes *did* owe more to Las Vegas than Polynesia. About halfway through the entertainment, Michi Hansen appeared. The manager had spent her evening thus far supervising the proceedings, and joined their table just in time for the hula contest.

Elizabeth Thomas immediately jumped up to take part. "Don't *you* dance the hula, Kaiulani?" she called out mockingly. "With a name like that, you should win hands down."

She's sure I would make a fool of myself, Lani thought angrily. She began to get up, only to feel Daniel's hand on her wrist, pulling her down again.

"No way," he said brusquely. "Not in that outfit . . . and not in front of five hundred people."

His protectiveness only goaded Elizabeth into further sarcasm. "That's right, Kaiulani," she cooed.

"Be a good little girl and do what big brother tells you."

"Lani looks charming," Michi interjected impatiently. "Really, Daniel, you're being impossible. Let her dance if she wants to."

He reluctantly released Lani's wrist and she followed Elizabeth to the stage. If anyone but Michi had dared to challenge Daniel's authority in such a manner, she thought, he would have squelched the offender ruthlessly. But Michi was very special, and as Lani danced she tried not to think about the rueful, tender look Daniel had given her as he complied with her wishes.

Lani had learned the graceful, seductive movements of the hula as a small child, and a determination to best Elizabeth Thomas loosened any inhibitions she might have had about publicly demonstrating her considerable expertise. Most of the mainland women were quickly eliminated, and eventually only Lani, Elizabeth and two others remained on the stage. As they danced, Jimmy Kent asked the audience to indicate its choice, with Lani the clear favorite. Elizabeth's look as she left the stage was pure venom, and Lani was rather shaken by it. Surely she had never done anything to deserve such antipathy.

"Would you folks like the lady to do a solo?" Jimmy Kent's question was greeted by whistles and applause, particularly from the male half of the audience. As Lani danced her eyes collided with Daniel's, and she wondered if his grim expression betokened some Fourth of July fireworks all his own. She devoutly hoped not.

Afterwards, Jimmy put his arm around her shoulder and said easily, "You look familiar, little lady. You dance the hula like a native."

"I am," she smiled. "You might have noticed me at your show a few weeks ago. I was with Mrs. Hansen and Mr. Reid."

A wolfish grin lit up the entertainer's face. "Well, now. I was going to award the prize myself, but I couldn't deprive my good friend Daniel Prescott Reid of that pleasure. Come on up here, Daniel."

Lani watched apprehensively as Daniel strode to the stage, the displeasure on his face replaced by a smile the moment he turned to the audience. Jimmy handed him an orchid lei and directed, "Give the little lady one of our special Hawaiian greetings, my friend."

Daniel shook his head. "I think the honor should go to my Uncle Charles. He's the senior member of the clan here tonight."

"How about it, Mr. Prescott?" Jimmy called out.

Charles Prescott stood up and boomed out in his gruff voice, "Wouldn't think of it! My nephew would never forgive me, Jimmy!"

Given the fact that every hotel menu, matchbook, and brochure read "The Maunalua Bay Hotel/A Prescott & Thomas Resort," it was not surprising that the audience quickly figured out that Daniel Prescott Reid and Charles Prescott were important company executives. They cheered and clapped as Daniel placed the lei around Lani's neck, kissing her lightly on each cheek as he did so. The next moment he was leading Lani from the stage, his hold on her arm far from gentle.

As the show continued, however, it seemed to Lani that Daniel's mood began to improve. By the time Jimmy Kent invited the audience to join in a community sing, he had unbent sufficiently to add his pleasant baritone to the proceedings. Lani had no idea why her participation in the contest had annoyed him, and didn't intend to ask. She was only relieved that as the last burst of fireworks faded from the moonless, starry sky, the incident appeared to be forgotten.

During the days that followed, Daniel was again gentle, considerate, and even-tempered. If some small part of Lani longed to provoke him into another demonstration of punishing domination, her common sense easily overruled such insanity. She would only end up badly hurt, and so would Brian, who was thriving under the tranquil atmosphere which reigned in the house of late.

On Monday, he had started day camp, along with several of the stepcousins who had befriended him at the luau. Lani began her regular job, her first assignment the prime minister of a small African nation. He and his wife appreciated Lani's fluent French as she catered to their primary interests: museums and old buildings.

She took them to the Mission Houses Museum, which included the oldest American building on the island. The house had been prefabricated in New England and shipped to the Sandwich Isles, the name bestowed on Hawaii by its English discoverer, Captain James Cook. It was then erected as a home for the first missionaries in 1821. The museum also housed a collection of mementoes of the missionary period of Hawaiian history.

Archeological exhibits and relics of the monarchy period were displayed in the Bishop Museum, where His Excellency was impressed by the spectacular crimson and yellow feathered capes worn by the Hawaiian kings. Lani then accompanied them as they toured half a dozen other palaces, churches, and tombs, and on Thursday dropped them off at the Governor's Mansion on Beretania Street, a building dating back to 1846, for a luncheon with top state officials. On a sudden impulse she decided to fill the resulting free time by inviting Daniel to lunch.

The guard in the lobby of his building was the same man Lani had met the previous week; he smiled and waved to her as she walked in the door. But as the high-speed elevator zoomed to the eleventh floor, Lani suddenly remembered her phone call to Daniel on the day his father had died, and the glacial manner of his secretary in refusing to put her through. If the woman persisted in acting like the leader of a defense squadron, what was she going to do about it? Make a dash down the corridor to his office and storm the fortress, unannounced?

There were two women at the reception desk: a beautiful brunette seated next to the typewriter, and an attractive, middle-aged redhead who was perched nearby, apparently issuing instructions. Both of them glanced up at Lani when she opened the door.

"Hello." Lani was aware of the nervous tremor in her voice. "Is Mr. Reid in? I'm . . ."

"You're Lani!" the older woman interrupted with puzzling enthusiasm. "There's a picture of you and Brian on Mr. Reid's desk," she added in response to Lani's bewildered look. "I'm Karla Darin, his secretary, and this is Gerry Ybarra, the division receptionist." She glanced at her watch and smiled. "Mr. Prescott is in with him at the moment, but they should be done soon. Let me buzz him and tell him you're here."

"Don't do that," Lani said hurriedly. "I wouldn't want to disturb him if he's with his cousin."

"Your scruples or my job," Karla said with a wince. "I was very sorry to hear about your stepfather," she went on softly, "and I'll never forget the day you called here. I'd been here for almost six months and Mr. Reid had never once raised his voice to me—even when I misplaced an important contract he needed. I know I should have recognized your name—he mentioned it to me the very first day I worked for him. But I forgot, and as soon as I realized what I'd done I went in to apologize and offer my condolences." Karla Darin shuddered quite visibly. "He was absolutely furious—I thought he was going to fire me on the spot. He chewed me out like a top sergeant, and when he was finally finished he picked up your picture and shoved it under my nose. He told me that if you ever came down here, I'd better recognize you."

Lani stared at her incredulously, finally managing to say weakly, "He must have been very upset. He and his father were very close."

"That's what I told myself, but whatever the reason, I hope to heaven it's never repeated. I was shaking for the rest of the day."

The secretary was reaching for the intercom when Daniel emerged from his office, accompanied by Richard Prescott. Both men smiled at Lani, Richard greeting her with a kiss on the cheek and a jovial, "Hello, my dear."

"Is everything all right?" Daniel asked.

"Fine. The Prime Minister and his wife are having lunch with the Governor. I had a few free hours, so I thought . . . if you're free . . . we might go out."

Daniel put his hand on his cousin's shoulder. "Richard, you've just witnessed the best offer I've had in weeks. May I take a raincheck?"

"Absolutely." He started toward the door, then called back over his shoulder, "Don't forget our golf game on Saturday. I aim to beat you for once."

Daniel took Lani to a well-known seafood restaurant

in Waikiki, suggesting that they order one of the house specialties: abalone, sliced paper-thin and served with a white wine sauce. When Lani expressed concern that her arrival had interfered with his previous plans, he shook his head and said warmly, "I have lunch with Richard once a week, but this is the first time you've indicated any desire to spend time with me. I'm very pleased by that, princess. I want you to be happy here."

Lani reached for her wine to hide the quick flush that rose in her neck, thinking how blissful life would be if only Daniel's feelings were romantic rather than platonic. Nonetheless, he was so charming to her that she soon found herself admitting many of the things she had hitherto kept to herself.

She told him that she was glad she had come to Hawaii; that she liked his family and enjoyed her job; and best of all, that she felt Brian was happy with his new friends and very much looked up to Daniel. He listened attentively, and although he refrained from uttering the mocking words "I told you so," his triumphant smile conveyed the message just as effectively.

"I suppose I can't blame you for gloating," Lani admitted. "I've given you a pretty hard time, haven't I?"

Daniel lazed back in his chair and grinned rather wickedly. "An understatement. If I'd known we were going to be fighting a cold war for the next seven years," he drawled, "I never would have kissed you so . . . thoroughly."

Lani was so embarrassed that she wanted to crawl under the table and never come out. Her eyes dropped to her empty plate as she considered a number of rejoinders to Daniel's beastly reminder of that horrible evening when she had been fifteen. Finally, desperately anxious to change the subject, she murmured, "The food here is very good, isn't it?"

"Only the best, princess," he said blandly. "How about some dessert?"

Mercifully, the conversation returned to safer topics.

By Sunday morning, Lani was contemplating that evening's dinner date with Robert Bradley without the slightest enthusiasm. She wanted no one's company but Daniel's, and if she hadn't known that he was escorting Michi to a dinner party, she would have fabricated an upset stomach and conveyed her regrets.

Rob phoned late in the afternoon to make arrangements, opening the conversation with the teasing statement, "I hope you realize that I'm using you, Miss Douglas."

"Using me?"

"You've been drafted as a chaperone. My daughter's birthday party is tonight, a barbecue and splash party. How do you feel about spending an entire evening with a few dozen maniacal high school students?"

Lani was delighted to help out. She might be too absorbed in Daniel Prescott Reid to provide amusing companionship at an intimate dinner, but surely she would be able to help supervise a group of teenagers. She knew that emotional longing and physical frustration were taking their toll in restless nights and troubled days, and suspected that boisterous physical activity might be the best thing in the world for her.

In fact, Dee Dee Bradley's friends were generally polite and well-behaved, but they were also ravenous and energetic. They ate like horses and swam like porpoises. Lani was wearing her tapa-print bikini under a terry-cloth shift, and eventually Rob coaxed her into joining the teenagers in a game of water volley ball. It was exhilarating fun to dive after the ball, and amusing to watch the antics of Dee Dee's friends. After several games she was out of breath and needed a rest, but was enjoying herself too much to leave the pool.

The ball was punched wildly back and forth across the net, great splashes of water hitting the concrete every time some six-footer flung his body in pursuit. And then one of those slabs of muscle and steel hit Lani. His head crashed into her stomach, knocking the air from her lungs. The last thing she remembered was fighting to stay above water, her chest burning fiercely as she struggled to take a breath.

She was unconscious only briefly, inhaling frantically as one of the boys pulled her from the water and handed her to Rob Bradley. "Easy, now," he said hoarsely as she panted for air. "You'll hyperventilate, honey."

Lani tried to slow her breathing as he carried her inside to his bedroom, but she had already begun to tremble and sob with shock. He sat down on the bed, cradling her on his lap, stroking her hair and murmuring to her as she cried against his shoulder. She realized vaguely that Dee Dee had come into the room with some clothing, exchanged a few words with her father, and then left.

Eventually Lani stopped crying, but still felt chilled in spite of the warmth of the room. "Dee Dee brought in some of her clothes for you," Rob said as she trembled against him. "Let me help you get them on, Lani."

"I can manage," Lani insisted. But when she slid gingerly from his lap and tried to stand, the room spun so wildly that Rob had to catch her in his arms and sit her back on his lap again.

"You *can't* manage. I'm going to help you." He reached behind her back and started to untie the double knot of her bikini.

"You can't do that," Lani gasped. "Ask Dee Dee . . ."

"I'm not leaving you alone. For heaven's sake, Lani, you almost drowned. I'm old enough to be your father, so stop acting like a child and let me help you."

Lani was too shaken to argue, meekly resting her head on his chest as he untied the bikini top, holding him around the waist for support. He tossed it on the bed, and reached for Dee Dee's polo shirt, gently pushing her upright. And then there was an explosion from the doorway.

"What's going on here?"

"Just take it easy, Daniel. I was helping Lani . . ."

"I can see what you were helping Lani to do, damn you!" Daniel bit out. "Get out of here before I deck you."

Rob gently transferred Lani to the bed, saying evenly, "You can apologize after you get the facts." Then he walked out of the room.

Lani held the shirt in front of her, stunned into silence by the extent of Daniel's rage. In seven stormy years she had never seen him look so angry. He stalked into Rob's bathroom and emerged with a long terry robe, which he threw at her almost viciously. Lani put it on, shivering from fright now as well as cold. She made no protest when Daniel lifted her into his arms and carried her out of the house to his car.

After several minutes she decided to risk an explanation, intending to begin with, "It isn't the way it looked." But she managed to get out only the first three words before he barked, "Just shut up!"

By the time he pulled his car into the garage, Lani felt much better. She was able to walk into the house without help, but then, Daniel offered none. As she climbed the stairs she could feel his eyes burning into her back, and she held the bannister like a lifeline, tensely making for the safety of her own room.

Before she had the chance to turn into the hall, Daniel was scooping her into his arms. He carried her into his bedroom and dumped her without ceremony on the king-sized bed. She bolted upright, hugging the robe around her body protectively and maintaining a wary silence, her eyes following his restless pacings up and down the length of the bedroom.

"You've known me for fourteen years," he said in a low, bitter voice. "Fourteen years! And every time I come near you, you either stiffen up like I repel you, or tremble like I'm some kind of monster." He stopped abruptly, his eyes frozen steel as they pinned Lani to the bed. "I thought I was finally getting through to you, but the second date with Rob Bradley, and there you are, letting him take your clothes off!"

"He wasn't taking . . ."

"The devil he wasn't!" Daniel's furious interruption sliced through Lani's hoarse protest. "Both of you half-naked . . . your arms around his back . . . your head against his shoulder . . . go on, tell me he was raping you!"

"Of course he wasn't . . ."

"I don't want to hear it!" Daniel barked angrily. His eyes never left her face as he stalked to the bed, but now the coldness was giving way to something far more dangerous.

Lani swallowed nervously to moisten her throat and

tried another appeal to his common sense. "I was in the pool, playing with the kids . . ."

"I said I didn't want to hear it!" And then he was beside her on the bed, pulling her roughly into his arms, turning her head, and lowering his lips to capture her own. When Lani tried to withdraw, his mouth hardened in retaliation. Lani went limp, forcing herself to offer no resistance even though her heart was pounding wildly with fear.

Daniel immediately released her and raised his head, and Lani, shaken to tears by his inexplicable attack, forced herself to open her eyes and look up at him. His mouth was twisted into a grim frown, his eyes defensive and tense. She considered another attempt at an explanation, then rejected it. Her protests only seemed to enrage him.

With frightening deliberation he reached over and clicked off the bedside lamp. Moonlight from a three-quarter moon filtered into the room; Lani stiffened as Daniel caressed her still-damp hair and in a gesture of bewildering tenderness bent his head to kiss the tears from each eye. "I'm sorry I hurt you, princess," he murmured huskily. His hand moved against her shoulder, pushing her back against the pillows, but Lani resisted by bracing her hands behind her. "Daniel, no. Please don't . . ." she pleaded.

In response, he shoved her so sharply that she sprawled onto her back, stunned by the disappearance of his gentleness. "Don't fight me," he said harshly. "If you do, I'll force you."

Passive resistance had worked before, so Lani tried it now. She lay motionless, almost numb with apprehension, as Daniel lay down beside her, opened the terry robe, and began to run his hand down her body, his mouth lightly nuzzling her neck. His touch was seductive but undemanding, and although she instinctively shrank away when he lowered his lips to her breasts, he appeared to take no offense at the withdrawal, but merely slid an arm around her back to hold her motionless.

It was impossible for Lani to ignore this method of arousal or hide the result. When both nipples were hard with desire, Daniel put his ear to her heaving chest to listen to the doubletime beats of her heart. Then he straightened, and said in a low, amused voice, "In five minutes I'll ask you if you want me to stop. You can always say yes, princess."

His promise was a potently effective bribe. Loving Daniel as much as she did, it was difficult for Lani to resist him in this gentle but insistent mood. A treacherous inner voice cajoled her to let him make love to her for just a few minutes more. He might never touch her again—was it so wrong to savor every sensation, save it up for the lonely days ahead? In any event, he had made it clear that she would be his prisoner for the next five minutes whether she fought him or acquiesced. Would it be so terrible to stop resisting and start cooperating?

His hands resumed their explorations, warm and firm and much too knowing on her body. His mouth wandered from her neck to her face, then settled atop her lips, kissing her with a sweet, irresistible tenderness. Lani tried to remember that his motive for seduction was anger, not love, but her emotions were swamping her common sense, her body arching against his hands, her lips moving responsively under his mouth, and her hands somehow reaching out to twine themselves around his neck.

Daniel turned on his side and pulled her close against

him, the hardness of his body igniting a blazing response in her own. She clutched at him convulsively and heard him moan, felt him shudder against her. Suddenly his mouth was urgent and demanding on hers, roughly parting her lips to probe the softness inside with a wildness that only heightened her arousal. She let him teach her how to move, everything blocked from her mind but an aching need to submit to whatever he asked of her.

When he tore his mouth away and growled hoarsely, "Well?" Lani could only moan his name. She had no idea what he meant. "Do you want me to stop?" he asked impatiently.

He might easily have taken her without the slightest protest on her part, Lani thought, her mind still somewhat muddled. But he had kept his promise and was seeking her consent, and that was something she could never give, not without his love. She whispered, "Yes . . . let me go," even though her enflamed senses cried out for exactly the opposite.

Daniel cursed under his breath and sat up, looking down at her with something very near hatred in his eyes. Then he muttered, "I've had it with waiting," and pulled Lani into his arms, his mouth covering hers with a painful possessiveness.

In that brief minute outside his embrace, Lani's sanity had reasserted itself. How could she have cooperated in her own seduction, all but making a gift of herself to a man who didn't love her? She wouldn't allow it to happen all over again. She pushed against his shoulders and tried to free her mouth, but Daniel dealt with her struggles as easily as a stallion swishing his tail at a fly. A moment later she was pinned impotently underneath him, her mouth aching from the brutality of his kiss. And this time when she stopped fighting and went limp, it only seemed to enrage him. His hand went to his belt buckle, frightening Lani into frantic resistance.

And then there was a ringing in her ears, and she knew she must be hallucinating from sheer hysteria.

Chapter Ten

The ringing continued for several seconds, insistently nagging at Lani's dazed mind until she realized that it was the telephone. The noise distracted Daniel as well; he froze just long enough for her to free one hand and grab the phone. No words would come out of her mouth, only the tortured, gasping sounds of utter breathlessness.

"Daniel? What's going on there?" the voice was Rob Bradley's, and as Lani tried to make some reply, Daniel snatched the receiver from her grip and muttered a brusque, "Yes?"

He was silent for a second, then said furiously, "What do *you* want?"

There was a second brief pause, during which Lani watched Daniel's expression change from fury to pure, white-faced shock. "She *what?*" he asked Rob, his voice as stunned as his face.

Now came a much longer period of silence. Daniel

sat with his head in one hand, muttering an occasional interjection but otherwise silent. When he finally spoke his voice was hoarse with torment. "I'm sorry, Rob. If you hadn't called . . . with Lani, I just seem to go crazy . . ."

And then Rob must have interrupted with some comment to relieve the tension, because Daniel smiled. "I intend to. Because you know what will happen if I don't." He paused, as if in thought, then went on, "A week from Monday. Be my best man, Rob."

Lani felt the color drain from her face. His best man? Whom did he plan to marry? Michi, as a buffer in this now-impossible situation? Or herself, out of guilt and perhaps physical infatuation?

Daniel hung up the phone and looked solemnly at Lani, who had been so intent on the conversation that she had forgotten that her robe still hung open. He reached over and closed it, tying the sash snugly around her waist.

"Near-drowning followed by near-rape. You've had quite a night." His tone reeked of self-condemnation. "I'm sorry, honey. When I found you with Rob, something just . . . snapped. And when you told me to stop, I couldn't . . . and I was furious that you *could.*" He shook his head in self-disgust. "This situation can't continue. We're getting married next Monday, and if I didn't have to go to New York tomorrow, it would be sooner."

Lani shook her head, almost overcome with pain because she would have to refuse to become Daniel's wife when every part of her ached for it. "I agree . . . we can't live in the same house any more . . . but there isn't going to be any marriage. This . . . this physical attraction between us isn't enough. There has to be love, too."

"It will come," Daniel said huskily. "Trust me, Lani."

She had given him a clear opportunity to tell her he loved her, but he hadn't. It hurt so badly that for a moment Lani felt physically ill, then a blessedly protective numbness set in. She shook her head again. "No. It's no good," she said firmly, astonished by her own calmness.

But this time, her objection only angered Daniel. "Stop it, Lani! You've been arguing with me for seven endless years. When are you going to admit that I know what's best for you?"

"Of all the arrogant . . ."

Lani's hot-tempered exclamation was cut off in mid-sentence when Daniel pulled her into his arms and lowered his head to kiss her. His mouth was gentle and persuasive, and by now her defenses were nonexistent. A spasm of desire burned through her, and with a groan she began to respond. After a few moments of tender yet thorough exploration he withdrew, saying in an amused voice, "That's how I plan to deal with your refusal. You have a choice, princess. Either you agree to marry me next Monday, or I take you without benefit of clergy. Right now."

Lani stiffened, feverishly searching for some way to make him see reason. "And . . . and what happened to that promise you kept making . . . that I'd be a virgin on my wedding night?"

"You will be, but first you have to agree to a wedding. When's it going to be, Lani? Now or next Monday?"

Suddenly it struck Lani that by next Monday she could be back in California, away from this whole excruciating situation. "All right, then. Next Monday," she said submissively.

Daniel grinned at her. "I had a feeling you'd say that."

Lani let him take her hand and lead her into his office, where he opened a wall safe, drew out several jewelry cases, and plucked an exquisite antique diamond and ruby ring from one of them.

"I've always . . . that is, I'd like you to wear this as an engagement ring. It belonged to my grandmother originally, then to my mother. I know how you feel about my family, but it would please me very much if you would accept it, princess."

Lani let him slide the ring onto her finger, greatly touched that he wished to give her something of such obvious sentimental value. "It's a little large, but we'll take it to the jeweler's in the morning," he said. "My plane leaves at noon. We'll have just enough time to pick up a license and choose wedding bands. I'll call my Aunt Marilyn and ask her to help you with arrangements. I'd like to be married here, by my minister, if that's all right with you."

Lani nodded, giving Daniel full marks for efficiency, especially in view of the fact that marriage could not possibly have entered his head until only minutes ago. And then he picked her up in his arms, carried her down the hall to her bedroom, and tucked her into bed. "Good night, princess," he smiled. "And sweet dreams."

Her dreams were anything but sweet. She lay awake for hours, unable to decide whether or not to go through with the marriage, and finally fell into a troubled, restless sleep. But by morning she had made her decision. She would pretend to go along with his plans until he flew to New York, then make her own arrangements to leave Hawaii. She knew that if she stayed on the island Daniel would track her down, and the next time he might not give her the option of a wedding ceremony. The ecstasy of his possession would only increase the pain of leaving him.

As for the pain of leaving Brian, Lani tried to put it out of her mind. She must do what was best for the child, and legal considerations aside, Daniel could give him a family, love and happiness, and great material benefits, while she could offer only years of struggle. Her alternative was to marry a man who didn't love her and live through the nightmare of waiting until his infatuation with her waned, and the marriage became a misery. Such a marriage would destroy her.

Daniel walked into her room the next morning with a teasing smile on his face. "For a newly engaged woman, you don't look too cheerful."

She mumbled something about a sleepless night. "Excitement, I guess," she added weakly.

Brian received the news of their engagement with all the nonchalance of childhood, observing in a bored voice, "I figured you were gonna get married. He always wants to hug you."

Somehow Lani made it through the morning without bursting into tears. Daniel's connections made short work of such formalities as blood tests and a marriage license. She asked him to choose their wedding rings, loving the matching gold bands he selected and cut to shreds by the knowledge that she would never wear her own.

"And now let's go tell Michi," Daniel said as he led her from the jewelry store in the Maunalua Bay Hotel. The beautiful manager was the last person in the world Lani wanted to see. How could she possibly maintain her fragile composure in the company of the woman Daniel really loved?

When Daniel announced the news to Michi his gaze was so tender and loving that Lani wanted to bolt from the room. The manager's reaction only confirmed what she had previously suspected. Daniel had accepted the fact that Michi was still grieving for her late husband and could not return his feelings; otherwise he would never have married Lani.

For Michi's delight could not have been anything but genuine. "It's about time! I'm happy she's finally putting you out of your misery, Daniel."

"Not until next Monday night," he answered ruefully. "This is going to be the longest week of my life." He kissed each of them good-bye and strode out of the office to catch his plane.

"Come sit down and have some coffee," Michi invited, her arm around Lani's waist. "On second thought, perhaps I should ring room service and have them bring some Bloody Marys. You look like you could use one."

Her gentleness was Lani's undoing. All morning she had forced herself to seem an eager bride-to-be, and now the tears she had so resolutely denied erupted uncontrollably. Michi led her to the couch and held her hand until she was able to stop. "Now tell me what all this is about, darling," she said. "Surely marrying a man who's absolutely wild about you can't be worth so many tears."

Lani stared at her, her tears for the moment forgotten. "He's not," she said huskily. "Daniel doesn't love me. I even told him that there had to be love as well as physical attraction, and he said . . . he said to trust him. That it would come."

"Obviously he assumed you were talking about your own feelings, not his," Michi scoffed. "Daniel has loved you for years." She paused thoughtfully. "But if he hasn't told you that, how did he come to propose?"

At first Lani was silent, too embarrassed to relate the events of the previous evening, but Michi probed until her weakened defenses gave way and the need to confide in someone overcame her innate reserve. She thought ruefully that Michi must be getting sick of listening to her sob her heart out.

But the manager gave no sign of impatience, merely shaking her head when Lani finished. "You're as stubborn as mules, both of you. I know Daniel. He's too unsure of himself to tell you he loves you unless you tell him first. And you do, don't you?"

Lani looked at her, astonished. Daniel Prescott Reid? Unsure of himself? It was impossible. Somehow Michi had received a completely false impression of his true feelings. "Yes, I love him," she admitted, "but . . . but he's in love with you. I've seen it . . . in the way he looks at you."

"How totally ridiculous! For heaven's sake, Lani, my husband and I were two of Daniel's closest friends. We were honored that he would confide in us about his feelings for you. Of course he's been a dear, dear friend to me since Keith died, and certainly we love each other, but only as friends." She paused, then smiled in that teasing manner of hers. "As a matter of fact, Daniel fancies himself a matchmaker. I admit I'm starting to think about new relationships, and since Daniel keeps extolling Rob Bradley's virtues, I just may decide to discover if all the propaganda is true."

"I think I'll take that cup of coffee now," Lani murmured. She was finding it impossible to believe what she was hearing. "You've never said anything," she reminded Michi. "Never even given me a hint you thought Daniel cared about me."

"Of course I did, in spite of the fact that he absolutely forbade me to say one word. The first day we met, I told you he had difficulty controlling his temper where you're concerned." Michi poured two cups of coffee and returned to the couch. "I made a point of letting you know how distracted he's been lately, and only last week, after Elizabeth had so charitably shared her poison, I told you that something had happened seven years ago to make him end their affair. Did I have to hit you over the head with it before you got the message?"

Lani felt herself blush fiercely, and tried to cover up her embarrassment by sipping her coffee. "You know about *that?*" she asked weakly.

"Of course I do. I told you, Keith and Daniel and I were very close. He was so shaken by his reaction to you that he stopped seeing Elizabeth. Of course that was before we met Daniel—we started to work for Prescott & Thomas about the time your mother died. It was almost a year before he told us anything about you, and by then he was completely in love with you. He thought you were wonderful, taking care of Brian and Jonathan, and more mature at sixteen than most of the older girls he dated out here. All the same, you were giving him a terribly hard time, and he wasn't about to let you walk all over him." She smiled in that teasing way that Lani found wholly charming. "I should like to have seen some of those arguments! Believe me, if Daniel had had his way, you would have been a child bride at eighteen, whipped into shape and permanently subjugated!"

"I don't understand," Lani said, finally beginning to believe that Daniel might really care for her.

"Jonathan wouldn't hear of it. He felt you were too young, that if he permitted Daniel to marry you, you would be under his thumb for the rest of your life. He insisted that you needed more time to mature, to become independent. Keith and I agreed. Daniel was wrapped up in his career and we pointed out to him that he could use the next four years far more profitably by concentrating on business and waiting until you graduated from college."

By now, some of Lani's natural spirit was returning, and with it, a touch of pique at Daniel. "What about *my* feelings? Wasn't that rather arrogant, to assume I would be ripe for the plucking?"

Michi only laughed. "Jonathan promised him that when you graduated, he would coax you into moving back to Hawaii. Daniel knew you were physically attracted to him, and he decided that with the proper gentleness, patience, and consideration, you were bound to fall in love with him!"

"Gentleness, patience, and consideration? He was like a steam-roller, flattening every objection I raised!" Lani protested, then added thoughtfully, "Of course, I was totally impossible, too. I even had defenses for my defenses. I didn't want to admit how I felt, and it scared me"—her eyes dropped in embarrassment—"the shameless way I wanted him."

"He felt the same way about you for years," Michi teased. "But when Jonathan died, it changed everything. The terms of his will were Daniel's insurance policy—he knew you would never leave Brian. Still, you resisted every move he made, and he was so frustrated by it that sometimes his temper got the better of him

175

and he simply exploded. In case you hadn't noticed, Lani, Daniel is a very emotional man." She permitted herself a mocking sigh. "If I have to sit through one more lunch or dinner with him, listening to him tell me that you're driving him insane, *I* may go insane. I have a hotel to run here. Speaking of which, we have a European prince and princess due in this afternoon, and a mainland bigshot next week. Do you suppose Daniel would mind if you skipped the honeymoon?"

"I don't think he would like that," Lani replied with a blush, "and I don't think I would either." Then she took Michi's hand and said, "I don't know how to thank you. You've done so much for both of us. I would be honored if you would be my matron of honor."

"Anything to get you two married!" Michi said with a twinkle in her eye.

Lani picked up Michi's visiting royalty from the airport at two o'clock that afternoon and took them for a drive around the Honolulu area, then settled them into their suite at the hotel. They would remain on Oahu until Friday, presaging a busy week for her.

When she got home Linda told her that Marilyn Prescott had invited her and Brian to dinner to discuss wedding arrangements. Daniel had informed his cousin that he wanted a traditional wedding with his family and friends present. Lani had envisioned a simpler, more private ceremony, but was happy to accede to his wishes. Nonetheless, she did ask defensively, "Do you think people will talk? I mean, it is rather . . . hasty." The spiteful face of Elizabeth Thomas flashed into her mind.

Marilyn's smile was reassuring. "On the contrary, we've all been expecting it. After all, Daniel has avoided serious involvements for years now, and it was obvious that he was waiting for *someone*. You were the logical young lady, and once we saw you two together, we began to wait for an announcement. One can hardly blame him for being in a hurry to marry you."

"About time you agreed," Richard added with a wicked glint in his eye. "I want my top executives working at peak efficiency, young lady. No wonder Daniel's been distracted, with you sleeping down the hall and your door firmly shut, I'll wager."

"Don't tease the girl, Richard," Marilyn scolded, taking Lani's arm and leading her to the staircase. "Come, Lani. I have something to show you."

"Something" turned out to be an exquisite Edwardian wedding dress, all delicate lace and seed pearls and yellowed silk. "It was originally worn by Daniel and Richard's grandmother Victoria. I'm saving it for my daughter Hope, but I know Daniel would be pleased if you would wear it."

For a fleeting moment Lani wanted to refuse. She had already accepted a ring owned by the frosty Victoria—must she wear her wedding gown too? But then she decided to lay the past to rest. "I'd be honored, Marilyn. It's beautiful," she said.

Before the evening was out, Tommy and Hope returned from a friend's house to offer their congratulations and help. "I had a feeling you'd wind up married to him," Tommy joked. "But I understand, if you couldn't have me, you decided to settle for second best."

Although Marilyn was handling most of the wedding details, there was still a great deal for Lani to do, and it filled her evenings. There were fittings for the antique gown, a shopping expedition with Michi to select a

177

bridesmaid's dress, and decisions about food, flowers, photographs, the wording of the ceremony, and physical arrangements for the wedding.

Daniel phoned twice, but because of the six-hour time difference from New York Lani missed both calls. He left the same message with Linda each time: "Tell Lani I miss her."

Late Friday morning she took the prince and princess to the airport, breathing a grateful sigh of relief. She finally had a few hours of free time, and decided to reward herself with a relaxing afternoon spent sunning and swimming at the hotel pool. It took ages to unwind, but finally Lani was able to doze off in her lounge chair.

She was awakened by some sixth sense that told her someone was standing and staring down at her. Her eyes flickered open—and looked up at the last person in the world she wanted to see.

"Well, well. Fancy running into you here," Elizabeth Thomas said, her tone making it clear that the meeting was no accident at all. "I have to congratulate you, darling. For a little mainland nobody, you certainly have hooked yourself a big fish."

"I didn't *hook* him, Elizabeth," Lani answered coldly. "He happens to love me." Silently she told herself that the snobbish Miss Thomas took after all the wrong people in her family.

"Does he? I doubt it. *Everyone's* talking about how he carried you half naked out of Rob Bradley's house. And in Rob's robe, no less. It doesn't take much imagination to figure out what happened next, does it darling?" She paused, then said maliciously, "How clever of you to trap him that way. Daniel *would* decide to do the honorable thing and marry you. He never could tolerate gossip."

Lani was shocked to learn that the incident appeared

to be common knowledge, but told herself that Elizabeth must be putting a unique interpretation on it. "I nearly drowned," she retorted. "I was chilled, so Daniel got me the robe. As for honor, if *that* was Daniel's motive, he would have married you seven years ago, wouldn't he?"

Elizabeth turned on her heel and stormed off, her nose in the air. Earlier in the week, Mrs. Thomas had conveyed the family's regrets—they were leaving for a vacation on Sunday. Lani had been grateful at the time, and now she was doubly so.

Although Lani was proud of the way she had dispatched Elizabeth, the vicious tirade put doubts into her mind. She had only Michi's assurances that Daniel loved her, and that wasn't the same thing as hearing "I love you" from Daniel himself. Her common sense told her that Elizabeth blamed her for her own failed romance with Daniel and was simply lashing out to hurt her or even stop the wedding, and yet her accusation made a certain sense. Daniel *could* be marrying her to protect her reputation, and the only way she would learn the truth was to ask him. She nervously awaited his return on Sunday, vowing that as soon as they were alone she would tell him she loved him and hope to hear the same declaration from *him*. Only then would she feel confident about their marriage.

But Daniel didn't return on Sunday. He called that afternoon to say that he had been forced to include a stopover in California, but would be home on Monday, well before the two o'clock ceremony. His voice was tender, concluding with a husky, "I miss you, princess," but he spoke no words of love and neither did Lani. She wanted to tell him in person.

Early the next morning there was a second phone call. "The plane has engine trouble, Lani, but they're trying to fix it. They may bring in another plane. I'll be home as soon as I can, on another flight if necessary." This time his tone was clipped and angry, so that Lani felt obliged to comfort him, teasingly reminding him that they couldn't very well start without him so they would just have to wait until he appeared.

The Prescotts arrived at one o'clock, Michi and Rob Bradley coming shortly thereafter. Lani told them about the latest delay, and Richard immediately called the airline. The plane had taken off an hour behind schedule, developed engine trouble, and turned back to Los Angeles. It was now due in at 1:40. Tommy went off to the airport with Daniel's wedding attire so that he could change while they waited for the luggage to come through.

Elizabeth's poison was never far from Lani's thoughts, and she would have been a nervous bride even without such last-minute problems. By two o'clock she was stalking around her room in her wedding gown, unable to sit down for fear of creasing it. How could she marry a man who might not love her? But then, with so many people downstairs, how could she do anything else? She refused Michi's offer of brandy because she hadn't been able to eat so much as a piece of toast all day, and knew the liquor was more likely to make her sick than calm her down.

Tommy's car pulled into the driveway at 2:30, and moments later Lani heard music from the piano—her cue that the ceremony was about to begin. "It's all right, darling," Michi told her. "You'll feel better once it's over with."

Lani had asked Richard Prescott to give her away. He met her at the foot of the stairs, taking her firmly by the arm and leading her to the far end of the living room where Daniel, Robert Bradley and the minister stood waiting. By now, she was dizzy from hunger and apprehension, so that the ceremony passed in a haze. Somehow she made the right responses, Daniel's arm around her waist providing the necessary physical support. Afterward, he kissed her lightly on the mouth, and Michi was right. She did feel a little better, because his smile had been so tender.

The buffet lunch was served outside in the garden. With Daniel by her side, Lani was able to eat something, smile, and enjoy the reception. Everyone told her that she looked the picture of a radiant bride.

Eventually, Daniel drew her aside and told her to go upstairs and change, they had an inter-island flight to catch, to Kona on the Big Island. It was nearly seven when they arrived at the hotel, and Lani longed to be alone with Daniel in their suite. Airplanes and public dining halls were not the proper places for a declaration of love, but Daniel had eaten almost nothing at the reception and wanted to have dinner immediately.

Their conversation was a continuation of what they had discussed on the plane: Daniel's business trip to New York and Lani's week at home. It was a strangely impersonal discussion for a newly married couple, and Daniel's offhand manner only served to make her more nervous and unresponsive. They had known each other for fourteen years, she thought in panic, and yet they were treating each other like strangers. She couldn't wait to get out of the dining room.

She barely touched her food. After dinner, Daniel asked her if she wanted to go dancing. "One of the hotels down the road has a good band," he explained.

Lani's taunted nerves snapped violently. "Couldn't we just go upstairs and get it over with?" she blurted out miserably. Daniel's eyes turned steel-cold, his mouth neutral. "I didn't mean . . ."

"It's all right," he said. "I understand how you feel."

When they reached the two-room suite, Daniel opened the door to the sitting room and walked through, then turned around. "Come get me when you're ready. I'll change in here." He all but slammed the door behind him.

You're really making a mess of things, Lani told herself unhappily. She slowly walked to her suitcase and opened it up, her eyebrows lowering in puzzlement when she spotted the box inside. She opened it; a sheer white nightgown was nestled in the tissue paper, a diamond and ruby necklace on top of it. The card inside read, "To my dearest wife, Lani."

It wasn't "I love you," Lani thought with a smile, but Daniel had obviously been thinking of her in New York, and that was encouraging. She held up the gown. It was an exquisitely sensual piece of froth, with lace over the breasts, criss-crossing in back but otherwise bare to the waist. The least she could do, Lani decided, was give Daniel a little encouragement of her own, no matter how edgy she felt.

She washed off her make-up, changed into the gown, turned out the lights and pulled back the covers of the bed. Then she opened the door and stepped into the sitting room.

Daniel was standing by the open sliding glass door to the balcony, dressed in a short terry robe, watching the sun set over the ocean. He didn't turn until Lani called out in a soft voice, "Thank you for the presents, Daniel. They're beautiful."

Then he swung around, the coldness in his eyes quickly replaced by a passionate, possessive look as his gaze traveled down her body. *"Hele mai,"* he said huskily. "Come here."

Lani complied, adoring the fact that he had addressed her in Hawaiian. She found it blissfully romantic. Daniel stood behind her, his hands on her shoulders, and murmured into her ear, "It's a beautiful spot, isn't it?"

It was. Black lava from some long-past eruption had flowed down into the sea, creating swirls of rock which now provided a home for tiny reef fish. Their balcony hung out over these crystal tidal pools; to the left was a black sand beach, and to the right a small garden. The sun was low on the horizon, casting a shimmering orange trail onto the water. Daniel ran his hands lightly down Lani's arms, then up again to her shoulders, and she realized in amazement that he was trembling—just as she was.

Their mutual silence only added to the tension. Daniel was making no move to make love to her, and she sought to cover her nervousness with light teasing. "What's the matter, Daniel? Afraid of losing your innocence?"

He turned her in his arms, his eyes soft yet intense. "No," he said hoarsely. "Nervous about taking yours. Afraid of hurting you." He paused. "And heaven only knows, after last week, you have reason to be afraid. I'll be as gentle as I know how to be, but for a woman . . . the first time . . . sometimes it's painful. No matter how careful the man is."

Lani twined her arms around his neck, her eyes misty from this sweet confession. "Oh, Daniel," she whispered. *"Aloha au ia oe."* The words meant, I love you, and he needed no further encouragement, picking her up in his arms and carrying her to the bed. Lani felt a

183

stab of disappointment when he failed to repeat the phrase back to her, but within minutes it seemed supremely unimportant. He aroused her with a tender expertise, stroking her body as if it were precious to him, kissing her with a controlled passion so intensely sweet she felt he could only be telling her he loved her with actions rather than words.

And she responded without hesitation, her body flowing against his like the molten lava that had once burned its way down from the mountains, her hands reveling in their right to explore his muscled hardness. She soon ached for more intimate contact and Daniel quickly sensed it, removing her nightgown and his own robe, murmuring, "You're so beautiful, Lani . . ." and then covering her body with his own.

Pain gave way to mounting excitement. Lani's total universe consisted of Daniel . . . his body taking hers, his hands caressing her skin, his mouth demanding a total submissiveness that she briefly withheld, then yielded. And when she was utterly pliant, a prisoner of what he was making her feel, he suddenly withdrew.

Lani clutched at him in confusion. Her protest was cut off with a kiss, his mouth rougher now, his hands holding her face and one leg pinning her body, refusing to let her get close to him. She ached for his touch—to be possessed by his body—and when at last Daniel complied, he excited her even more wildly than he had the first time. She moaned, a hoarse, unbidden sound deep in her throat, and wanted to scream with frustration when he left her again.

"Daniel . . ."

"Shhh. It's all right," he whispered, mercilessly teasing her mouth, thwarting her attempt to come back into his arms.

Lani had never felt so totally helpless in her life . . . like a marionette, with Daniel pulling the strings. This ruthless domination seemed to have nothing to do with love, but he had aroused her so completely that she had no choice but to lie quiescent and let him do whatever he wished with her. When he again covered her body with his own and renewed his tantalizing conquest of her senses, she heard herself make the same moaning sounds as before, only now she couldn't stop.

Daniel lifted his mouth. "Lani?" he whispered.

"Please, Daniel," she pleaded, almost in tears. "Don't torment me . . ."

He lowered his head again, and now there was no more teasing—only compelling movements of his hands and body that brought shudders of fulfillment to both of them.

Afterward, Lani lay on the bed, emotionally exhausted, and watched as Daniel walked into the other room, returning with an ash tray and lit cigarette. She was deeply distressed by the way he had made love to her. What had been the point of it? Her total humiliation? Her abject surrender?

He lay back down on the bed and said conversationally, "I gave up smoking years ago, but I still crave one of these after making love." He kissed her lightly on the mouth. "I have the feeling this honeymoon is going to be very hard on my lungs."

Then, aware that she hadn't even smiled at the joke, he asked in a concerned voice, "What's the matter, darling?"

When she was silent, he coaxed, "C'mon, Lani. I know I didn't hurt you. I thought you enjoyed that. Please tell me what's wrong."

"It's just . . . the way you . . . why did you do

that?" she stammered, tears streaking down her face. "Why did you have to make me feel so . . . so helpless?"

Daniel stubbed out his cigarette and gathered her into his arms. "Hey, don't cry, princess. I never meant to upset you. I just wanted to please you." He drew slightly away so he could look into her eyes, and smiled—a crooked, sheepish little grin. "Okay, that's not entirely true. I admit I wanted to impress you with my skill as a lover. My ego was involved—I wanted to arouse you so completely that you'd forget any other guy who ever touched you. But try to understand . . . I've fantasized about this moment for nearly seven years, Lani. I wanted it to be . . . fantastic."

Lani stared up at him, not knowing what to say. Finally she whispered, "And was it?"

"For me, yes. Because when you add deep love to intense physical attraction, you . . ."

"What did you say?" Lani interrupted instantly. Was Daniel finally telling her what she longed to hear?

"I said, 'When you add deep love . . .'" He paused, then grinned down at her. "You think I haven't told you that, huh? Except I have, a hundred different times over the last six years, by trying to help you, to spare you pain, and even by my jealousy. But you refused to see it." His voice dropped in pitch and became more tender. "If you were more experienced, you would know that a man doesn't make love like that to humiliate a woman or dominate her. I wanted to give you as much pleasure as I could, partly because it was exciting for me, but mostly because I love you."

He pulled her back into his arms, and Lani willingly snuggled closer. "And to think I almost ran out on you," she mused.

"You *what?*"

"I did. I didn't understand why you wanted to marry me. I thought it was lust, or concern for my reputation, or unrequited love for Michi." She felt a rumble of laughter against her chest. "Well, I did. And I ended up in tears in Michi's office, and she told me . . . well . . . everything."

"Did she?" he demanded. "Did she tell you that you've been driving me crazy ever since you were fifteen? When I saw you in June you were still a kid. By August I couldn't keep my eyes off you. I was appalled at myself—and half-insane from your constant teasing. I knew the last thing in the world I should do was go off in the car with you, but I couldn't stop myself, any more than I could help kissing you. The only way I could rationalize it was to pretend that I was teaching you a lesson, but afterwards I knew I couldn't react that way to you and still marry Elizabeth. Then your mother died, and my father had a heart attack, and you were so brave . . . and strong, and caring . . . I fell head over heels, in spite of how young you were. There were times when I wanted to turn you over my knee for being so stubborn, and every time I saw you I had trouble keeping my hands off. I was jealous of every guy you dated, including my good friend Rob Bradley, who I could have cheerfully murdered the night I found you two together. Did Michi tell you all that?"

"Not exactly," Lani admitted. "Just that you've been in love with me for years, and that you wanted to marry me when I was eighteen. But then," she added softly, "I've been keeping you at a distance, convincing myself that you were arrogant and brutal, manufacturing resentments against your family, and ranting on about your company, all because I didn't want to admit I felt the same way."

Daniel leaned back against the pillows, gently pulling Lani down beside him. "Keep saying things like that and you'll be trapped in this hotel room for the next six days, princess. The only part of the Big Island you'll see is the view from our balcony, and our only contact with the outside world will be when I call room service for our meals . . . and more cigarettes!"

"We could always come back," Lani giggled.

But Daniel's attention was no longer on the conversation. He played with a lock of her hair, then ran his hand down her side to her hip. "I want to make love to you again," he murmured, his lips against her neck.

Lani started to turn into his arms, then changed her mind. "No," she stated firmly. "Not now."

"What do you mean, no?"

"I mean N period, O period. No." She started to get up, only to be pulled back down. She pushed against Daniel's chest, trying to escape his hold, but he was having none of it. After a breathless tussle she found herself imprisoned by his body, her arms captured above her head.

"You're going to pay for that bit of rebelliousness, Mrs. Reid," Daniel threatened.

When Lani made no reply, he bent his head and kissed her, a bruisingly passionate exploration of her mouth that left her hungry for more. When he lifted his head and saw the desire in her eyes, his expression became quite objectionably complacent.

"I want you, and I'm going to have you. You understand that, princess?"

"Yes, Daniel," Lani answered meekly.

"Are you going to fight me?"

"No, Daniel." She paused for just a minute, then

added poutingly, "But I'm not going to beg. Not ever again."

"Is that supposed to be a challenge, Mrs. Reid?" he drawled.

"Yes, Daniel." Lani smiled, and proceeded to let him prove her a liar.

READERS' COMMENTS ON SILHOUETTE ROMANCES:

"You give us joy and surprises throughout the books . . . they're the best books I've read."
—J.S.*, Crosby, MN

"Needless to say I am addicted to your books. . . . I love the characters, the settings, the emotions."
—V.D., Plane, TX

"Every one was written with the utmost care. The story of each captures one's interest early in the plot and holds it through until the end."
—P.B., Summersville, WV

"I get so carried away with the books I forget the time."
—L.W., Beltsville, MD

"Silhouette has a great talent for picking winners."
—K.W., Detroit, MI

* names available on request.

Silhouette Romance

ROMANCE THE WAY
IT USED TO BE...
AND COULD BE AGAIN

Contemporary romances for today's women.

Each month, six very special love stories will be yours

from SILHOUETTE.

Look for them wherever books are sold

or order now from the coupon below.

$1.50 each

— # 1 PAYMENT IN FULL Hampson
— # 2 SHADOW AND SUN Carroll
— # 3 AFFAIRS OF THE HEART Powers
— # 4 STORMY MASQUERADE Hampson
— # 5 PATH OF DESIRE Goforth
— # 6 GOLDEN TIDE Stanford
— # 7 MIDSUMMER BRIDE Lewis
— # 8 CAPTIVE HEART Beckman
— # 9 WHERE MOUNTAINS WAIT Wilson
— #10 BRIDGE OF LOVE Caine
— #11 AWAKEN THE HEART Vernon
— #12 UNREASONABLE SUMMER Browning
— #13 PLAYING FOR KEEPS Hastings
— #14 RED, RED ROSE Oliver
— #15 SEA GYPSY Michaels
— #16 SECOND TOMORROW Hampson
— #17 TORMENTING FLAME John
— #18 THE LION'S SHADOW Hunter
— #19 THE HEART NEVER FORGETS Thornton
— #20 ISLAND DESTINY Fulford
— #21 SPRING FIRES Richards
— #22 MEXICAN NIGHTS Stephens
— #23 BEWITCHING GRACE Edwards
— #24 SUMMER STORM Healy

— #25 SHADOW OF LOVE Stanford
— #26 INNOCENT FIRE Hastings
— #27 THE DAWN STEALS SOFTLY Hampson
— #28 MAN OF THE OUTBACK Hampson
— #29 RAIN LADY Wildman
— #30 RETURN ENGAGEMENT Dixon
— #31 TEMPORARY BRIDE Halldorson
— #32 GOLDEN LASSO Michaels
— #33 A DIFFERENT DREAM Vitek
— #34 THE SPANISH HOUSE John
— #35 STORM'S END Stanford
— #36 BRIDAL TRAP McKay
— #37 THE BEACHCOMBER Beckman
— #38 TUMBLED WALL Browning
— #39 PARADISE ISLAND Sinclair
— #40 WHERE EAGLES NEST Hampson
— #41 THE SANDS OF TIME Owen
— #42 DESIGN FOR LOVE Powers
— #43 SURRENDER IN PARADISE Robb
— #44 DESERT FIRE Hastings
— #45 TOO SWIFT THE MORNING Carroll
— #46 NO TRESPASSING Stanford
— #47 SHOWERS OF SUNLIGHT Vitek
— #48 A RACE FOR LOVE Wildman

Silhouette Romance

__ #49 DANCER IN THE SHADOWS Wisdom

__ #50 DUSKY ROSE Scott

__ #51 BRIDE OF THE SUN Hunter

__ #52 MAN WITHOUT A HEART Hampson

__ #53 CHANCE TOMORROW Browning

__ #54 LOUISIANA LADY Beckman

__ #55 WINTER'S HEART Ladame

__ #56 RISING STAR Trent

__ #57 TO TRUST TOMORROW John

__ #58 LONG WINTER'S NIGHT Stanford

__ #59 KISSED BY MOONLIGHT Vernon

__ #60 GREEN PARADISE Hill

__ #61 WHISPER MY NAME Michaels

__ #62 STAND-IN BRIDE Halston

__ #63 SNOWFLAKES IN THE SUN Brent

__ #64 SHADOW OF APOLLO Hampson

__ #65 A TOUCH OF MAGIC Hunter

__ #66 PROMISES FROM THE PAST Vitek

__ #67 ISLAND CONQUEST Hastings

__ #68 THE MARRIAGE BARGAIN Scott

__ #69 WEST OF THE MOON St. George

SILHOUETTE BOOKS. Department SB/1

1230 Avenue of the Americas
New York, NY 10020

Please send me the books I have checked above. I am enclosing
$_____ (please add 50¢ to cover postage and handling for each
order. NYS and NYC residents please add appropriate sales tax).
Send check or money order—no cash or C.O.D.s please. Allow six
weeks for delivery.

NAME_____

ADDRESS_____

CITY_____ STATE/ZIP_____